SAPPHIRE ICE

Book 1 of The Jewel Series

by

HALLEE BRIDGEMAN

Published by
Olivia Kimbrell Press™

Olivia Kimbrell Press™

COPYRIGHT NOTICE

PUBLISHED BY: Olivia Kimbrell Press™*, P.O. Box 470, Fort Knox, KY 40121-0470. The *Olivia Kimbrell Press™* colophon and open book logo are trademarks of Olivia Kimbrell Press™. *Olivia Kimbrell Press™ is a publisher offering true to life, meaningful fiction from a Christian worldview intended to uplift the heart and engage the mind.*

Some scripture quotations courtesy of the King James Version of the Holy Bible. Some scripture quotations courtesy of the New King James Version of the Holy Bible, Copyright © 1979, 1980, 1982 by Thomas-Nelson, Inc. Used by permission. All rights reserved.

Words and lyrics from the hymn, SOFTLY AND TENDERLY JESUS IS CALLING, in the public domain. Words & Music by Will L. Thompson, originally published in Sparkling Gems, Nos. 1 and 2, by J. Calvin Bushey (Chicago, Illinois: Will L. Thompson & Company, 1880)

Original cover art by Amanda Gail Smith (www.amandagailstudios.com).

Library Cataloging Data

Names: Bridgeman, Hallee (Hallee Bridgeman) 1972-

Title: Sapphire Ice; The Jewel Series book 1 / Hallee Bridgeman

254 p. 5 in. × 8 in. (12.70 cm × 20.32 cm)

Description: Olivia Kimbrell Press™ digital eBook edition | Olivia Kimbrell Press™ Trade paperback edition | Kentucky: Olivia Kimbrell Press™, 2012.

Summary: The men in unbeliever Robin Bartlett's life have only ever been users. Believer Tony Viscolli's arrival and relentless interest in Robin both infuriates and intrigues her.

Identifiers: ePCN: 2017900419 | ISBN-13: 978-1-68190-044-5 (trade) | 978-1-68190-045-2 (POD) | 978-1-68190-074-2 (hardcover) | 978-1-68190-046-9 (ebk.)

1. Christian romance fiction 2. man-woman relationships 3. suspenseful love stories 4. sisters family saga 5. sisterhood relationships 6. redemption faith grace 7. marriage holy matrimony

PS3568.B7534 S277 2012 [Fic.] 813.6 (DDC 23)

SAPPHIRE ICE

Book 1 of The Jewel Series

by

HALLEE BRIDGEMAN

To: Amanda
Live a life of love.
Eph 5:2

Hallee Bridgeman

DEDICATION

For My Darling Gregg...

THERE aren't words to adequately express my love and appreciation for you. I am so happy God brought us together, and I look forward to forever and ever.

TABLE OF CONTENTS

 PROLOGUE

There were three of them. Sisters. Half-sisters, technically, born to the same mother but different fathers. They lived in bad circumstances, the kind of childhood existence that makes for melodramatic and heart-wrenching movie of the week scripts. Some nights were bad, and then there were those nights when it was really bad. The really bad nights they all had to hide.

Tonight was one of those really bad nights.

Robin hadn't gotten out of the way fast enough. Maxine and Sarah had been able to hear her screaming from their closet hiding place, but to go out there, to face him wouldn't have helped Robin. It would have just given him two more targets, or possibly hostages. Eventually, Robin crawled in with them, shaking with fear and rage, not even knowing which was the strongest emotion from one tremor to the next. She'd managed to fight him off this time. He was probably still trying to get his breath back. However, Robin needed her strength for the next day... and the next... and the one after that.

Blonde, blue-eyed Robin was fifteen. The oldest of the three, she acted as their protector. She had no memory of her father but knew he was doing seven to twenty-one for trafficking cocaine.

Twelve-year-old, green-eyed Maxine had olive-skin, with straight, dark hair that testified to the proof of her father's American Indian blood. A warm bed on a drunken night, only Maxine's features gave evidence of which of her mother's many one night stands had fathered her. She had never learned his name. Neither had her mother.

At nine, little Sarah had a small frame and could easily pass for six. Her brown, curly hair had red streaks that came out in the summer. She needed glasses, but he had already broken them twice, so she suffered in a blurry world. Before her second birthday, her father had played lollipop with a loaded revolver and lost.

Robin wrapped her sisters in her arms as they heard the front door open, heard their mother's raucous laughter and a man's answering voice. Then HE started yelling and the sound of breaking glass made each girl flinch.

Their mother's shrill shrieks added to the cacophony, and a new man's voice joined in. The three girls inched farther back into the closet as the fight intensified. Shouting escalated. Words became clearer. Robin tried to cover her sisters' ears to block out the quarrel. The adults screamed at each other about a deal gone bad, about drugs, about money. There had been many fights like this in the past, and the three sisters prayed that he would leave this time.

Sarah screamed at the sound of the gunshot. Robin grabbed her and covered her mouth with her hand. Greasy fear churned through her gut at the sound of another shot.

And another. And another. Four shots in all, then a deafening, roaring silence that screamed in their small ears.

In the silence, Maxine shifted, but Robin gripped her arm tight enough to bruise, her dirty nails digging into her sister's brown skin. Heavy boots moved through the apartment, entered their room, started toward the closet. They each drew in a breath and held it, not even wanting the sound of their breathing to give them away. Then the screech of sirens penetrated the thin walls and they heard the heavy boots run, heard the door slam.

They didn't move. They waited through the silence, through the banging on the door, through the dozens of footsteps that entered the apartment. They heard the shouts and the buzzing and chirping of handheld radios. They heard the metallic clicks of hammers falling back onto unfired chambers and eager, stiff muzzles sliding forcefully back into worn leather sheaths. They heard muttered curses about wasted lives or scumbags slaying scumbags. The light in their room flicked on and, after a moment, a voice called, "Hey, Sarge! There's toys in here. Little girl toys. Dolls and stuff."

They sat there in the dark, quivering with their backs to the wall, their arms wrapped around each other, and shivered together, terrified of what waited for them outside the closet.

CHAPTER ONE

The wait for a table at Hank's Place spilled out beyond the patio and into the parking lot. Parents stood in cliquish groups, tightly gripping little trophies, pagers for tables, and various beverages from the bar. Throngs of little leaguers dashed around chasing each other, exactly as loud and somewhat rowdy little boys ought to do. They wore white jerseys with yellow sleeves, each bearing the Hank's Place logo, which accounted for the presence of such a large crowd on the last night of the season.

Robin Bartlett balanced her tray over her head and stood on her tiptoes to keep from losing her balance as a pack of nine-year-old players shoved by her. A yellow cap landed at her feet and, with dexterity, she slipped her toe under it and kicked up, catching it in midair as she continued forward with the drinks. She arrived at her target group of parents and delivered two diet colas, an iced tea, and a water with lemon without dislodging a single drop.

"Do you know how much longer we'll be?" A perfectly

groomed and well-bejeweled mother asked, irritation heavy in her tone.

Robin smiled, feeling the headache she'd fought all evening start spearing the back of her right eyebrow. "We're setting up for you in the outside bar area," she answered. Number seventeen bumped into her, knocking her sideways. Seeing a head bare of a cap, she placed the cap in her hand atop the tawny head and gave the bill a quick tug. "Shouldn't be more than five or ten minutes."

The customer pursed her lips but didn't say anything. Robin stepped slightly to the left and addressed the next group clustered around the large potted fern. "Would you like something from the bar while you're waiting?"

One of the women in the group answered. As she shoved the designer sunglasses on top of her head, the diamond tennis bracelet on her tanned wrist caught the light of the setting sun. "We're a church group."

Robin bit her tongue before she blurted out exactly what she thought of "church groups" and instead smiled a bright, saccharine smile. "I can get you water or cola from the bar as well."

The woman actually looked Robin up and down, from the toes of her worn out black sneakers to the top of her tightly bound blonde hair. Once she had concluded her inspection, she turned her back as she spoke, as if dismissing Robin. "No, thank you."

Robin shrugged it off without offense. She met a dozen like her a day. She worked her way through the crowd, taking drink orders and reassuring parents that the wait wouldn't be much longer. Some were rude, some polite. Robin guessed the polite ones had once waited tables. It didn't matter either way to Robin. Robin's boss paid her simply to fill drink orders, not make lifelong friends.

After making her way back into the restaurant and behind the bar to pour wine and beer, she paused for just a moment to roll her head on her neck, trying to relieve some of the tension. She caught her reflection in the mirror behind the bar. She wore her blonde hair wrapped into a tight bun at the base of her neck. That style unintentionally accented her high cheekbones and long neck and helped the casual observer focus on her deep blue eyes and long lashes. She wore makeup only to hide the shadows under her eyes and the cheeks pale from fatigue. She wore the standard bartender uniform of Hank's Place, with her starched white shirt and black slacks, which helped to exhibit her too-thin waist and long legs.

She'd worked in the bar for eight years. Hank had given her the job at eighteen, and from the first day she'd had to fight off the men who made passes on an almost nightly basis. The regulars eventually learned that a date could not be had, and also attained an education on just how badly fingers could ache for days as the consequence of a casual touch. As the years went by, she occasionally felt tempted to take one of them up on the offer for a date, but the truth of the matter was that she didn't have time. She didn't have the time for a date, and she certainly didn't have the time for a man in her life.

Robin simply worked. She slept, ate, and worked. She methodically made drinks and served customers. She was the head bartender now, and while she could have done without the added responsibility, the extra pay helped. The little bonuses Hank slipped into her paycheck from time to time let her know that he appreciated her and the regular crowd who managed to find their way in only on the nights she worked.

Two hours later, her hands burning from the bleach water used to wash the glasses and her feet feeling like they might just fall off, the restaurant reached its peak dinner time. The hostess told the people at the entrance that the wait would be at least an hour if not more and the customers, to Robin's continuing surprise, accepted that. Happy hour came to an end and the rush of double orders ended, so Robin just concentrated on keeping the waiting customers happy and keeping the eating customers served. That worked for her because her headache beat against her skull in a thundering rhythm that she kept expecting nearby people to overhear.

Regardless, her smile looked fresh to the new customers who had sidled up to whatever free spot they could find along the bar, and she fixed their drinks with the same efficiency as she had two hours earlier. She took money, pocketed tips, and offered an audible, "thank you," as a mother carted out a toddler who had screamed for the last forty-five minutes. She turned toward the cash register and barreled into the solid chest of Hank Lamore. Even though she stood nearly six feet tall herself, she barely reached his shoulder and had to crane her neck to give him a grin.

Hank ran his place as tightly as he'd run his ship when he'd served as a Captain in the Navy. Even though he edged toward sixty, discipline over his body and the daily workout regime he put himself through kept him looking early forties. Robin owed him almost everything.

"Break, Robin," he stated flatly in his gravelly voice.

She snorted and skirted around him, not even bothering to respond.

He turned and snatched the bills out of her hand and stepped between her and the cash register. "I said break. And I mean a full half hour. Not the measly five minutes you try to get away with."

If she sat down for a full half hour, Robin knew she'd fall asleep. Still, she'd learned not to argue with the boss. She'd get off her feet for a few minutes, drink a cup of coffee, maybe take an aspirin, and then get back to work. Hank might growl at her then, but he wouldn't try to force the issue.

With cup in hand and a be-right-back wave to her regulars, she went through the double doors off to the side of the bar into the kitchen. Casey stood at his place behind the huge stainless steel table, inspecting plates and passing or failing them with his very high standards of sensory appeal. Those approved went onto the warmer shelf in front of him where the wait staff lingered, waiting to pick up their orders. Those rejected got whisked away back to the minions behind him who then scurried to make repairs and please the legend. Chef Casey stood very short and very thin, thin enough that it always surprised Robin that he could even lift the larger pots off the stove.

He gifted Robin with the grimace that passed for his smile, making his uneven teeth flash startling white against his ebony face. "Hiya."

Robin smiled back, "Hiya yourself." She headed to the corner of the big room toward a large table that sat ready and waiting for the staff to sit and relax on their breaks.

"Alright, then."

The ritual greeting hadn't changed over the past eight years. With a sigh, Robin leaned back in the chair and propped her feet in the one across from her. "How's the world treating you, Casey?"

"Well, now, here and there, mostly." A plate with a ten-ounce steak, mushroom risotto, and some fresh vegetables artfully displayed on the side made it to the finish line. Once Casey topped it with herbed butter, a waiter immediately snatched it up and put it on his tray. "You'll be wanting some of my pie to go with that coffee."

"I would, yes." She'd offer to get it, but she knew not to enter the stainless steel kingdom. The regular staff—regular meaning anyone not trained in the art and craft of preparing fine cuisine—remained relegated to the large oak table in the corner. Casey had used the same table for *mise en place* back when Hank's was nothing more than a glorified one-room burger joint.

She watched him dice some green herbs with such speed and precision that it made Robin's aching head spin. He sprinkled them into a large stainless steel pot and tasted his sauce before he fixed her a slice of pie. Without asking her, he went into the large freezer and returned with two generous scoops of vanilla ice cream on the top, then served it to her with exaggerated movements. "Not quite the fancy feast you used to getting at that Benedicts'."

Sighing around her spoon at the taste explosion of the perfectly seasoned apples, Robin could only shake her head. When her tongue finally quit enjoying long enough that she could use it to form words, she chuckled. "They've got nothing on you, Casey. Not a darned thing."

His cackle followed him back to the stove. "Not a darn thing," he laughed while he glanced through a tray of raw aged steaks awaiting his approval before they could have the honor of searing to juicy perfection on the grill.

Neither spoke again. Casey concentrated on perfection

while Robin concentrated on quickly devouring as much of the pie as she could. Waitresses and waiters came and went, bringing empty plates to exchange for full ones, too busy to have a conversation during the circle. It didn't bother Robin, though. She enjoyed the quiet, broken only by the opening and closing of the swinging doors.

One of the bartenders, Marissa, pushed open the door and stuck her head through, scanned the kitchen, then looked back behind her. "She's in here."

Robin had just pushed her plate away and started to contemplate getting back on her feet when she looked up and watched her sister Maxine stalk through the doors into the kitchen. "What are you doing here?"

Maxine laughed and glided to the table. She wore some green little sparkly sheath looking thing and shoes with such heels that Robin wondered how she stood without toppling over. Robin had heard people refer to her sister as beautiful all her life, but as adolescence gave way to adulthood, she thought that the word stunning might better apply. Her jet black hair fell thick and straight to her hips. She stood tall and thin with a delicate figure Robin would have gladly traded for her more generous curves. Her most striking feature was her eyes. They were green, nearly emerald, slightly slanted in the corners with lashes so long and full they required no helping enhancements by way of mascara.

Maxine pulled the chair out from under Robin's feet and sat down, propping her chin in her hands. "I have a date. He's meeting me here."

Robin glared at her sister while she contemplated actually getting back on her feet to step out the back door for a quick breath of fresh, Boston air. "You have to work tomorrow."

Maxine glared right back. "So do you."

"That's different."

"How?"

Robin sighed and rubbed her forehead. "Because I'm working now. I'm not out late playing so that I'll drag into work tomorrow and have to come up with new ideas on too little sleep."

Maxine sat back in her chair and crossed her arms over her chest. "I've been telling you for a year, Robin, to let me help you, now. You don't have to work two jobs."

"I'm not taking your money, Maxi. You work hard for it, and you deserve to be able to have things."

Maxine grabbed the hair on either side of her head and tugged while she groaned out loud. "Listen to yourself! You've done nothing but sacrifice since the day I got out of high school, and you're talking about me deserving to have nice things! When is it your turn, Robin?"

"Sarah finishes school in two years."

"You put me through four years of school, set me up with a contact from Benedicts', and expect me to sit back and make twice as much money as you and not contribute?" She slapped her palm on the top of the table. "That's nonsense."

Robin took a pull of her coffee and set the cup down hard enough that it should have broken. "You wouldn't be having this conversation with me if I were your mother instead of your sister."

"Well, you aren't our mother. Besides, don't bet I wouldn't. You're twenty-six years old. By the time Sarah finishes, you'll be nearly thirty. That's when you decide to start living your own life? Almost thirty years old and never even been on a date?"

Temper surged through Robin in a white flash. She looked into her sister's face, a face that looked nothing like her own. "I refuse to measure the quality of my life based on the number of men I've dated. I will not be like her, dating thirty men by the time she was thirty. Relying on a string of boyfriends for survival, then being shot to death by one of them. Whoopee! Life was one big party."

Robin stood, put her hands flat on the table, and leaned forward until her face was close to Maxine's. "I don't need a man in my life like her to feel my life is complete. I've managed to put you through college, our sister halfway through, and if I accomplish nothing else, I will have done more than I had ever dreamed possible. I get great joy out of seeing you successful in advertising, as I'll get when I see Sarah as a nurse. If it means that I sacrifice my youth, then so be it. Neither one of you will ever have to rely on any man for your livelihood, either."

Maxine stared at her for a second, then started laughing. "Is that what this is all about?" She rose from the chair until, in her heels, she stood taller than Robin. "Sis, you can have fun with a man, go out on a date, relax, enjoy yourself, and not have to rely on him for your livelihood. You're allowed to do that."

Robin grabbed the cup and drained the rest of the coffee with one swallow. "I don't need it and I don't want it. My life is good, now."

"Your life is work!"

"Work and you two. It's honest. Clean. I don't need anything else."

"You don't know that!"

"I've seen the other side, Maxi. I'm not going there."

Maxine stepped back and took a deep breath. "Okay. I'm not going to try to argue with you anymore. But, will you do one thing?"

She moved to the back door and Maxine followed. "What's that?"

"Will you go to college when Sarah's done? Will you let the two of us help you do that?"

This time, she laughed. "Yeah, right. That's a good one. Me, the high school dropout, go to college at thirty something."

Maxine squeezed her shoulder and turned to leave. "You're the smartest person I know, Robin, and you deserve to be happy."

She pushed the door open with her shoulder and stepped into the cool night air. "I'm happy."

"No. You're just happier. There's a big difference."

Robin snorted. "Go do whatever it is you do on a date. But try to make it an early night. You have to sell tires or something tomorrow."

"Ha-ha. Actually, it's peanut butter. We need to convince choosy mothers to choose a different brand."

Robin plunked down on an overturned crate and stared at the gravel on the ground at her feet long after her sister left. She looked up at the night sky, gazing up at the stars she could see through the haze of the city lights. Finally, shaking off the dark mood that apparently came out of nowhere, she went back into the kitchen to find Casey waiting for her with a bottle of aspirin and a glass of water. She smiled as she took them from him, then swallowed two of the pills.

"That Maxi. I've always liked that one." Taking the bottle and the empty glass from her, he turned away, heading back to roost. "Smart girl."

Robin stretched her lower back. "Shut up, Casey."

His cackle followed her out of the kitchen.

At seven-thirty that night, Antonio "Tony" Viscolli opened the door to Hank's Place. He'd done his research. He always did his research. He knew that Thursday nights were the busiest weeknight at Hank's, just as he knew that Tuesdays and Fridays were the busiest days for lunch, and Saturdays were the busiest nights on the weekend.

He didn't plan this visit. In a spontaneous move, he stopped in on the way from the airport. Tony wanted to know if he would like or dislike the business without them knowing they had a potential buyer peeking under the carpets. He'd liked what he'd seen on paper. He'd liked what he'd heard on the street. He really liked what he saw when he walked into the building.

The house was packed with families. Somehow, despite the understated elegance and four-star menu, it came off as a family place. That surprised Tony. He expected the same stuffiness found in fine dining all over the city.

"Impressive," Barry Anderson said from well above and right beside him.

"Very," Tony replied, moving forward toward the smiling hostess, his towering companion at his side.

"I like it," the giant offered. "I really like it."

The hostess explained that there would be a short wait and directed them to the bar area. Tony stood an even six feet tall, with the stereotypical dark olive complexion that most every Sicilian sported, and dark brown eyes set in a lean, angular face. Still, even at six-feet, he only came up to Barry's shoulder.

People mistook Barry's size to mean that he worked as Tony's bodyguard, and the men had shared plenty of laughter over the assumption. He stood at six-nine, weighed close to three hundred pounds of steel hard bone and muscle, with sandy blond hair and ice blue eyes. The massive Super Bowl Ring on his massive right hand sparkled in the low lighting.

Barry served as Tony's attorney and had done so from the very first business deal Tony had made that required a lawyer. His practice had grown, as Tony's business had grown, until it was one of the largest law firms in the city. While Barry oversaw his own practice with due diligence, he—and he alone—only ever personally handled Viscolli business.

The bar area was busy for a restaurant bar. When a cheer rippled through the bar, Tony glanced up and saw the possible reason for the crowd. A Red Sox game played on the large flat screen television gracing the wall opposite the bar, and the boys had just pulled ahead.

Two stools became available at the end of the bar. Within thirty seconds of sitting down, a bartender appeared in front of them. She handed the man on the other side of Barry a fresh beer, and as she brought her hand back, she pulled the levers on the tap in front of her to fill another two glasses.

"What can I get you gentlemen?" she asked as she Frisbee tossed cardboard coasters in front of them.

The second her eyes collided with Tony's, he felt like

something sucked all of the air out of his chest. She had crystal blue seas for eyes that he somehow knew would drown him if he let them. Shaking his head to ward off whatever unexpected sensation had suddenly struck him, he cleared his throat and gave her his order. "Ginger ale with lemon."

"And you, sir?" she asked, her eyes sliding over to Barry.

"Shirley Temple."

Tony had to give her credit. Most bartenders did a double take whenever Barry ordered. She simply nodded and began to prepare their drinks.

"Hey, Robin. No way will you know this one," the man on Tony's left spoke.

If he hadn't found himself so intrigued and closely observing her, he wouldn't have spotted the flicker of annoyance before she laughed and set his drink in front of him. "I'm telling you, Sandy, give it up."

"No way. I got you this time." The man laughed and pounded the bar with his fist. "Straight Law Cocktail."

Her hands never stopped working while she answered. "Gin and dry sherry." She added an orange slice and a few extra cherries to the glass and set it in front of Barry. "Stirred, not shaken."

An elbow nudged Tony's ribs, making him slosh his drink. "That girl. She's the best."

"Is she?" Tony asked rhetorically, then helped right the man before he sopped up the spill with his napkin.

Robin reached across the bar and took the rest of Sandy's drink. "That's it, hon'. You're done."

"Come on, Robin. At least let me finish my beer."

Her eyes remained sober through her smile. "Sorry, Sandy. You're falling off the stool as it is."

"You can't just cut a man off at the knees like that."

Tony watched with interest as she handled the intoxicated man next to him. She set a mug of black coffee in front of him along with his tab, called a cab, made two more drinks, collected Tony's money for their drinks, and all the while talked to the inebriated man, teased him, kept him happy while he waited for his cab.

Tony could have watched her work all night. The longer he watched, the more he realized that he wasn't the only man in the building upon whom she had such an effect. Several knew her, stopped to speak with her, and more than one stared at her with the same desire Tony felt skirting at the edges of his mind. It irritated him that he could fall so easily into line with a dozen others, and he frowned into his drink while he considered it.

"Well, well. Antonio Viscolli." He looked behind him and saw a man who could easily rival Barry in size. His head was shaved, he sported a mustache and a partial beard, and had tattoos running up both arms. "You officially checking me out Mr. Viscolli?" he asked with a laugh.

Tony grinned and held out a hand. "Hank Lamore. It's good to see you again."

"You should have told me you were coming out. I'd have held a table."

"We were coming in from the airport and decided to swing by." He gestured to his right. "Barry Anderson... Hank Lamore."

Tony caught one more look at the bartender as she worked farther down the bar before he set his full attention to the matter at hand. "Do you have an office, Hank?"

"Sure. Come on back."

On the way to the seller's office, Tony pushed the blonde out of his mind and turned it fully and completely to the business at hand.

CHAPTER TWO

A t five-thirty, **the shrieking** of the alarm clock finally penetrated the thick fog of sleep that Robin had savored for too few hours. With a groan, she rolled over and hit the button to silence the stupid thing, then forced herself into a sitting position.

She put her elbows on her knees and rested her face in her hands. Three hours of sleep would get her through the day, but just barely. Hopefully, she'd still get a chance this afternoon to take a nap before she had to be back at Hank's.

With a yawn, she rubbed her face and stood up. She had to be dressed and at work in forty-five minutes. She stumbled through the darkened apartment, passed the closed door of the room that housed Maxine and Sarah, and into the tiny kitchen. She stopped short when she saw Sarah already at the table, nursing a cup of tea.

"Why are you up so early?" she mumbled, fumbling for a coffee cup, sloshing in the rejuvenating brew that had percolated to perfection the last twenty minutes of her sleep time via the wonderful invention of a timer.

"I have a test at seven-thirty."

Robin collapsed into one of the two remaining chairs and stared at her sister through half-open eyes. Sarah had always been petite and almost delicate, but on the verge of adulthood, she looked nearly angelic. She wore wire-rimmed glasses that subtracted nothing from her hazel eyes. Her hair fell to her shoulders, an auburn mass of curls that no amount of styling could contain, framing a small face sprinkled with freckles. She'd barely breached the five-foot mark, with such a delicate bone structure that Robin sometimes worried a strong hug could break her.

In two more years, she would receive her bachelor's degree in nursing, and Robin wondered how she'd ever have the stamina to make it through the rigors of the education process. Whenever that particular thought materialized, Robin made herself realize that Sarah had always been tougher than she looked. They all had. Robin just had to constantly remind herself of that fact.

"Why are *you* up so early?" Sarah asked in return. "Seems like you just got in."

A yawn made Robin's jaw pop, and she had to wipe the tears from her eyes before she spoke. "There's a Chamber of Commerce breakfast at the club this morning."

Sarah arched an eyebrow. "Isn't Benedicts' a little fancy for a Chamber breakfast?"

Benedicts' was a very private, very exclusive dining club, and very picky about not only the patrons, but also who worked on staff. She'd applied every two months for three years, but it was one of the most sought after restaurant jobs in the city. The summer before Maxine started college, Robin finally managed to secure a job at

Benedicts'. She worked the lunch shift six days a week, and on a slow day made a hundred in tips. She'd been able to put Maxine through college on her tips alone, and managed to save enough from her hourly paycheck at Hank's for the year that she had to pay the tuition and books for both Maxine and Sarah.

She yawned again. Two more years. Then she could rest. "There's some member who's sponsoring it, paying for the whole thing." Which probably meant scrimpy tips, but it would still amount to more than she could earn bagging groceries for two hours, and that made it worth it.

"Are you working lunch, too?"

"Just the first shift. I have to be at Hank's at six, so I'm taking off at one and sleeping for the afternoon."

Sarah rose to add more water to her cup. "Oh, that reminds me. Can you get some of Benedicts' artichoke dip?"

Robin had her head on the table, quietly dreaming of being back in her bed. "Probably, why?"

"Mom is having some church something or other. I told her I'd try and get her some."

Sarah sat back down as Robin kept her face hidden. She just felt too tired to fight her emotions and didn't want her all too perceptive little sister to recognize the pain that must have flashed in her eyes. It felt like a knife twisting in her heart.

Unlike Robin and Maxine, Sarah made it through the system found a home with a real family. An older couple who'd tried for years to have children of their own had just recently applied for and been approved for foster care. Sarah went to them that terrible night. They'd fallen in love with her, and immediately went through the motions to make her theirs. Even though Sarah had older sisters, they made it understood that they could only manage one child.

They felt very protective of Sarah and, because she had no memory of anything until that very first morning in their home, they cut off all ties to her past including her half-sisters. Robin fought for visitation rights and the courts finally granted monthly visitation after Sarah turned fifteen. Robin and Maxine sat in the Thomas kitchen and drank coffee for one hour a month while reacquainting themselves with their little sister. Every single visit, Sarah's adopted mother hovered near the door unabashedly eavesdropping the entire time.

Because the Thomas couple couldn't afford to send Sarah to college on their retirement income, Robin approached them. She offered to fund Sarah's college on the condition that her youngest sister had to move in and live with Robin and Maxine. At first, the Thomas' flatly refused. Ultimately, their concern for Sarah's future forced them to accept Robin's terms, but they made it clear that the acceptance came grudgingly.

Robin didn't care. Finally, all three sisters came back together again. Except no matter how she tried to bridge the gap, she had neither the bond with Sarah that she shared with Maxine, nor the closeness that should have come naturally to sisters, even half-sisters.

She knew no small amount of jealousy fueled the emotion that besieged her whenever Sarah talked about her foster parents, which in Robin's mind bordered evil. She felt jealous that Sarah had found a home and knew what it was like to get a hug before bed instead of either nothing or a slap across the face. She had a functional, intact family, complete with grandparents and uncles and aunts and cousins, of which Robin and Maxine never would and never could claim as their own.

Robin swiftly stood and gulped her coffee down. "No problem. I'll check with Carmine and see what I can get."

"Thanks, Robin. You're the best."

Once again, she wore her hair in a tight bun. Sometimes, she just wanted to cut the whole mass so that she wouldn't have to deal with continually putting it up for sixteen hours a day. Except that every time she started, her hands paused on the scissors and she couldn't bring herself to do it.

Her makeup looked perfect, her lipstick crisp and even. She wore another starched white shirt, tighter and more feminine looking than the one she wore at Hank's, and a short black skirt with dark stockings. A bow-tie hugged her neck, and she draped a trim black apron with white pinstripes around her waist.

Working at Benedicts' required a good memory. The wait staff did not carry a notepad and had to memorize every order perfectly. Carmine, the general manager, felt that notebooks served as a crutch and took away the necessity for eye contact with the customers, creating too informal of an atmosphere. That required the staff to also memorize any specials, details about all of the dishes (is that made with peanuts?), and the extensive wine list.

Thankfully, Robin had a good memory. It sometimes surprised her, considering the quantity of drugs her mother had consumed on a regular basis, that the three sisters had been born with any brain cells at all. Pure necessity forced Robin to drop out of high school, but she'd always loved to learn. Unfortunately, she never had time to read anything but the daily specials and any book that came out that listed new drinks, and she imagined that's why she found it so easy to remember everything else.

"You look a little piqued this morning, Robin," Stan Humphrey observed, fiddling with his tie at the mirror in a corner of the kitchen. The dress code did not allow for clip-on ties, and Robin finally brushed his hands away and fixed it for him.

"Three hours of sleep will do that to you."

He stood tall and lanky, sporting dull brown hair speckled with gray and flat green eyes on a face Robin always thought of as uninteresting. At times she liked him, and at times he gave her the creeps. She remembered enough to know the signs of habitual drug use. "You partied last night?" he asked with a grin.

No one knew of her other job. The management here frowned on any kind of moonlighting, and they operated under the guided assumption that she'd left her position at Hank's to work exclusively for them. "Ugh! If I never see another rum and Coke again, it'll be too soon."

He leaned closer to her ear and she had to restrain the urge to flinch back. "I have a little pick-me-up if you're interested."

She raised an eyebrow and kept her voice at a normal level. "You ever offer me drugs again, Stan, and I'll probably have to break one of your fingers."

He slouched back, holding up both hands as if to ward her off. "Okay. Sorry. You just looked like you needed something. No offense meant."

"Well, it was taken."

"Robin. Stan. Take your posts, please." The *maître' de's*

voice rang out in a singsong sound through the kitchen. "Okay, people," Clarence continued, "we have a buffet available, but our guests may order from the menu if they prefer." He looked at his pocket watch as ten waiters and waitresses brushed by him and headed toward the doors that lead to the dining room. "The bar is open, and Billy is ready with pitchers of Bloody Marys and screwdrivers. Mimosas are available with our normal champagne list." He clapped his hands together twice. "Serve well people."

Robin stopped near him to grab a silver coffee pot. "How did we manage to get the early shift, Clarence?"

He winked and whispered conspiratorially. "Tell me about it. I have my lunch patrons' whole lives memorized, but I only know half the people out there." He looked over her head toward the head table. "Boston's royalty is here."

Robin felt too tired to even be intrigued by Clarence's abnormal awe. "Maybe we can get Stanley a jester's hat," she whispered back, then pushed open the door to the dining room and forced a serious expression onto her face. The door swinging shut cut off his choking laughter.

She had rarely seen the dining room so packed with people. They had closed the restaurant for the meeting, and it surprised her to see so many people there. However, it occurred to her that most of this morning's customers didn't enjoy membership at the exclusive club and wouldn't get many opportunities to dine at Benedicts', especially for free.

Clarence knew she had waited on some of the head table diners as regular lunch patrons so he assigned it to her to serve. She addressed those she knew by name and tried to discretely read the name tags of those she didn't recognize. Methodically, she worked her way down the long table, pausing to chat when required, fetching drinks as needed.

"Mr. Riley, it's good to see you again. I think it's been several weeks," she said, speaking to the president of the Chamber.

"I've been on vacation, Robin. Have you ever been to Italy?"

She smiled and filled his coffee cup. "Not yet, but I want to go someday. It's on my bucket list."

"Beautiful country, dear. If you ever get the opportunity, don't pass it up."

"If a trip to Italy ever falls into my lap, I'll remember your advice." She moved to the next person while Riley continued to speak.

"Tony, if you've never had Robin here serve you, you've been missing out on the best that Benedicts' has to offer."

"Yes. I think I've heard something similar about her before."

The smooth voice sounded almost familiar, but she couldn't quite place it. She took her attention from the cup and lifted her head, her gaze meeting a pair of black eyes that, somehow, seemed to look all the way inside of her, instantly learning all her secrets. "I didn't expect to see you here," he said.

"Do I know you?" She asked, her voice soft, almost a whisper. At the last second, she lifted the coffee pot before she overfilled the cup.

He kept his voice as soft as hers. "Not officially."

"I'm sorry, I don't…" her eyes skimmed his name tag, "I don't recall meeting you, Mr. Viscolli."

His teeth flashed white against his olive skin. "I unofficially met you last night."

Panic skirted up her spine and she looked around the room. Lowering her voice even further, she leaned closer so that he could hear her. "Please, don't say anything. I... we can't... I mean, another job..."

He placed a hand on her wrist, startling her. His hand felt rough, but warm. Warm enough that it sent heat up her arm, moving to flush her face. "So, what you're saying is that your job may be in my hands."

The heat in her body turned to white hot anger. "Release me, sir." She bit out.

With a smirk, he cocked his head as if examining a specimen. "What would you do to keep your job, I wonder?"

It took every ounce of training and skill she had learned from years in the service industry to maintain her cool facade. With an even voice, she said, "I don't play those games, Mr. Viscolli. Remove your hand, or else I'll remove it."

He shifted his grip until his fingers encircled her wrist. They overlapped on the thin bones, and this time he did chuckle. "You think you could?"

In a panic, knowing how long she had spent serving this customer, she glanced up and spotted Clarence watching her. Baring her teeth, she leaned close to the man's ear and whispered. "I can and I have, on men bigger than you. Are you willing to test me?"

With a grin, he reluctantly let her go. "Perhaps another time I'll take you up on your challenge."

Unable to stand the thought of leaving him with the last word, she leaned forward again, barely speaking above a whisper. "If the thought of seeing you again didn't repulse me, Mr. Viscolli, I'd almost look forward to it."

With that she moved on down the table, ignoring his chuckle that followed her parting shot. She found it especially challenging to keep a polite smile on her face and make inane chatter with the other patrons as she continued to serve while seething inside. How dare he?

She headed back into the kitchen to get more coffee and Clarence immediately intercepted her. "Did you have a problem with that man, Robin?"

Out of earshot of the customers, she slammed things around, surprised that she didn't dent the silver coffee pot. "Nothing I couldn't handle," she said, slamming the top back on her serving container.

He gripped her elbow and kept her from reentering the room. "I know that sometimes customers might get a little—well—fresh with some of our girls, but I wouldn't want to think that you might have—albeit unintentionally—insulted one of them."

She bared her teeth at him. "Did he look insulted?"

"No, but you looked insulting, and I'm concerned because I've never seen you act that way before."

She slammed the coffee onto a counter and stepped closer, until she could poke his bony chest with her finger. "I didn't like the way he looked at me, I didn't like the way he touched me, and I didn't like what he implied when he spoke to me." When he flinched, she realized how hard she poked him and stepped away from him, drawing in a deep breath to calm down. "Now, you've had your little 'chat' with me. Do you intend to speak with him?"

Clarence's face fused with color. "Robin, do you have any idea who that is out there?"

"I don't quite have the approbation for most of our patrons as you do, because I truly don't care." She grabbed the pot of coffee and pushed open the door.

He took insult at her words, as she intended, though she regretted it the second his face fell. She paused and went back into the kitchen. As she opened her mouth to retract it, he straightened, stiff as a board, and put a regal tone in his voice. "That is Mr. Antonio Viscolli. He is one of the stockholders of this club, and is hosting this morning's breakfast. If you would like to lodge a formal, written complaint, I will entertain reviewing it, but in the meantime, you are here to serve, so I suggest you return to your post." He looked her up and down, his expression hinting that he didn't much care for what he saw. "Unless, of course, you'd like me to have someone else wait the head table. I'm sure that any server out there would be happy to trade places with you."

Oh, what a tempting notion. She considered it, very seriously, for several breaths. Ultimately, she decided that trading tables would most certainly give Viscolli a great deal of satisfaction, a game point. No, she'd serve him, and do a heck of a good job at it. "That won't be necessary, sir. I'm fully capable of performing all of my duties."

His face softened, momentarily. "I know. Now, get back to work."

Not wanting to leave things tense with someone she considered a friend, she paused to make one of her normal parting remarks. "Purple and green," she said. At his confused look, she continued, "with bells. For Stan's hat."

His mouth twitched as he fought the smile and waved her away.

CHAPTER THREE

Barry gripped the side of the golf cart to keep Tony from tossing him out as he took a sharp turn, and asked, "Have I ever told you how much I loathe this game?"

"It's a necessary evil. I doubt very seriously that much business could get done in a football huddle." Tony skidded to a stop at the next tee.

"How long have we known each other?" Barry asked superfluously as Tony leaped from the cart and snatched the number two driver out of the bag strapped to the back of the cart.

Tony chuckled and took a practice swing. "Too long for you to ask that question."

"In all that time, you've never—I repeat—never, done business on a golf course."

"Sure I have. I've formed relationships, negotiated deals, worked out problems—"

Barry cut him off by laughing. "You could get as much

done over a lunch or dinner in half the time. You just want the excuse to be outdoors."

"Maybe," he said with a smile. Tony lifted his face to the sun and breathed deep. "But look at this sunny day! You look like you could use some fresh air anyway, buddy."

In a few short weeks, the skies would loom dark and overcast, sending flurries of snow that would hamper driving, keep people indoors, and dampen spirits. The thought brought memories of shivering in the doorway of an abandoned building at age seventeen, two weeks after his mother's death. He'd survived, thrived even, but he hated winter. He normally retreated to his home in the Florida Keys during those cold months. Recently, however, and all too often, business interfered and forced him to stay weeks at a time in the chill climate of the North.

Today Bean Town enjoyed unseasonably warm weather. The bright blue sky and crisp air gave him extra energy, and he wanted to take advantage of it one last time. He'd met with Barry immediately after the Chamber breakfast, not even going to his office first. The way the day had started to shape up, and with the air growing warmer by the minute, he had no intention of going in at all.

He stood back as Barry teed off. The ball landed perfectly in the middle of the fairway, just off the green. "I don't know why you hate this game so much. You've just about mastered it."

Barry threw his driver into his golf bag and watched Tony hit a nearly identical shot. "There's no challenge." He grinned and climbed back into the cart. "And very little blood."

"Ahh. Honesty." He followed the cart path until they reached the green. "Barry, I've been thinking. I want Hank's."

The two men climbed out of the cart and chose their clubs. "Tony, I don't think it's a good idea."

Tony looked at the club in his hand. "You think the pitching wedge instead of the nine iron?"

"Ha, ha." Barry offered drily. "Seriously, Hank is who keeps it alive. He has that touch. Without him, I think it's going to lose whatever it has that makes it so special and become just another restaurant."

"He's going to sell it, anyway." He watched as Barry lightly hit the ball, smiled as it rolled to about two feet past the hole.

"Good. Let someone else take the loss."

A scowling face with a pair of bright, deep blue eyes hovered in front of Tony's vision. Then he remembered her body, her grace, her grin.

"No. Give him his asking price but give him some earnest money up front. Ten percent, maybe. That's in addition to the asking price if he stays on as manager. That will keep it Hank's."

"His asking price? You could probably cut it by at least twenty percent."

Tony's ball landed on the green and slowly rolled toward the hole, teetered on the edge, then fell into the cup. He turned his body and looked directly at Barry, his face hard, his eyes serious. "Barry, I have accountants. I need you to be my lawyer. Think you can get the papers drawn up today?"

Barry shrugged before he putted. "It's your money."

His ball rattled into the hole. "What about the bar?"

Tony retrieved his ball from the cup. "You know I don't like it. None of my other restaurants have a bar. I'll have to think on it and pray on it, but I'm already ninety percent sure we'll lose the bar."

"With Hank wanting to keep his staff, we'll need to make sure something that extreme is in the contract."

"Whatever you need to do." Tony watched as Barry retrieved his ball and they both replaced their putters and climbed back into the cart. "See, Barry? You're wrong again."

"Again? About what?"

"I just conducted business on a golf course."

"True. But it would have been more satisfying if I could have tackled you to the ground with my bare hands instead of whacking some stupid little ball with a stick."

Tony chuckled for the sake of the gentle giant's sense of humor. He always laughed at Barry's jokes. The men understood each other on many unspoken levels. They approached the eighteenth hole. "As soon as we're done here, I'll buy you lunch," Tony offered.

Barry sighed, obviously understanding that lunch would likely be the day's special at Hank's Place. He pulled his telephone out of his pocket and dialed his office number. "I'll have the papers waiting on us. We'll need to stop by my office on the way."

The three men sat in Hank's office in the back of the restaurant, sandwiches at their elbows. Hank had reading glasses perched on his nose and slowly read over the contract one more time. "What's the deal, here? Did someone find uranium under the patio tiles? Am I sitting on top of an unknown oil well or gold mine?"

Tony drained his glass, uncommonly relaxed. "Yeah," he drawled, "your restaurant. This place is its own gold mine."

Hank looked at him over the rim of his glasses. "Don't play games with me, Viscolli. You have a reputation that well precedes you and I'm not as dumb as I look. How come you're giving me my asking price without even trying to negotiate?"

Tony returned his stare. "I want to buy this place. You want to sell it."

"What's this offer of earnest money above the asking price? This ties me in for five more years if I accept it."

Tony shrugged. "It's pretty black and white. Why the questions?"

"Because, suddenly, I don't trust this deal."

"You contacted me, Lamore. I've done my due diligence and this is the only way the place remains profitable."

"What does a small-time restaurant outside the city limits have that draws the direct attention of the infamous Antonio Viscolli?" He tossed the contract on the desk in front of him and leaned back in his chair. "I sign nothing until I figure that out."

Barry spoke. "You sell nothing if we get up and walk out, too."

Hank shrugged. "Maybe not to you, but I will to someone, and probably inside of five years."

Tony surged out of his chair and paced to a picture

hanging on the wall. He stared at a picture of a younger Hank, looking very different in a crisp white uniform, his arm draped across the shoulders of a woman, presumably his wife, standing in front of their restaurant. A banner across the front of the building read "Grand Opening."

He put his hands in his pockets and rocked back on his heels. "I want to buy this place for the reason that I buy anything—because it's a moneymaking venture. I'm choosing to offer you your asking price for two reasons. First, it is actually a very reasonable asking price, and you could have asked for more. You should have consulted with more people before locking in. Secondly, I like you. I rarely allow emotions to affect business deals, but I do like you, and I figure my offer just might make your retirement sweeter." He crossed the room and stood near his chair, but didn't sit. "I'm not going to play cat and mouse games with anyone. You decide, now or in your own time, but you decide without the games."

Hank drew his glasses off and rubbed his eyes. "I have a condition that I absolutely will not back away from."

Barry uncapped his pen. "What's that?"

"You keep my employees, without pay cuts and with similar benefits."

"That's a standard clause. If you'll see article fifteen of the—"

"I don't need to read it. I'll take your word." His eyes cut to Tony but addressed Barry. "Because I'm guessing your word is as good as his."

"The bar will be removed. The bartenders will have to be assigned new jobs, and if they choose to quit instead, that will be their choice and not affect the contract."

Hank raised an eyebrow. "No bar?"

Barry answered, thumbing through the stapled contract and marking places requiring his personal touch. "No Viscolli restaurant has a bar. We're also closed on Sundays in observance of the Sabbath."

Hank looked from Barry to Tony. "No kidding?"

Tony gave a slight nod of his head. Hank continued. "Okay. That's intriguing." He cleared his throat. "I'll sign these papers in two weeks. It will give my lawyer time to go over them, and give my wife time to make sure that it's what we want to do."

Tony held his hand out. "Then we'll be in touch in two weeks."

Antonio Viscolli rarely took an entire afternoon off. It often felt like that wherever he went, whatever he did, business followed, and when business followed, it meant dealing with people: asking, demanding, meeting, negotiating. If it wasn't a lawyer, it was a secretary. If it wasn't a secretary, it was a reporter. On and on, constant demands. He didn't necessarily dislike or resent it, he accepted it as his life. Even at church, people needed, demanded, requested.

He woke early daily to pray and meditate on God, to read his Bible, and to have conversations with his heavenly Father. Because of the norm, he considered the opportunity to get away in the daytime, during business hours, a rare treat.

After working almost nonstop for months, Tony felt fatigued. He couldn't remember a time his energy felt so diminished, but when he thought back, he realized hadn't truly taken any time for himself for a couple of years. The golf game relaxed him a bit, but he needed more. He needed to pour some energy into something, let his body slow down with his mind.

He needed to sweat.

He'd taken up rowing because kids with his background didn't row. It was a sport in which the blue bloods of the country competed, kids in Ivy League schools and their recent graduates. It brought him one more step away from his childhood, one more step closer to discarding his past. It also required no interaction with another human being. He had a tendency to treasure his solitude.

He let his mind wander as the muscles in his arms worked the oars. Smoothly and cleanly he cut across the water, letting the sun beat down on his head, warming his neck and shoulders. The breeze blew warm, heated by the late summer the state presently enjoyed, and he lifted his face, letting the stress and pressures bleed out of him with each stroke.

In just two short weeks, he would celebrate his thirty-second birthday. All he had striven to achieve in life had been accomplished and then some. He found himself very nearly bored. Perhaps he needed to set his sights on something new. Something that didn't require contracts or negotiations. The water reflected back at him, as blue as a pair of eyes that hadn't left his mind in nearly twenty-four hours.

Pushing the thought away, he tried to plan for the coming month. He'd spent almost too much time in Los Angeles, but it had been necessary. It had taken him some time to establish himself in the business, to make sure those he left in charge considered him the ultimate boss. It had taken a lot of work, but he had friends who helped him out, helped him sort through the lingo and nuances unique to Hollywood. With their continued help his company would provide good, quality, Christian films and television shows, and it would soar.

Because they all did, all the enterprises he owned. Tony Viscolli insisted on it.

A bird flew by overhead, hunting fish foolish enough to swim close to the surface. He heard it cry out, watched it circle back, then dive down and come up clutching its dinner in its beak. Across the river, he passed a small boat with a father and son fishing. The oars occupied his hands, so he nodded to return their polite wave, glad no words needed exchanging. If envy twisted in his gut at the sight of such a simple father and son outing, he ignored it and pushed the feeling away, focused on something else.

Women had often thrown themselves at him. He knew he was physically attractive and actually used his looks to his advantage as he scrambled up the ladder of success.

When it had become necessary, he'd hired consultants and learned how to dress immaculately for whatever the occasion demanded. He'd learned how to speak without his street accent coming through, learned what fork to use when, and learned how to have polite dinner conversation. He had transformed himself, but his Savior had transformed him even more completely before Tony ever began that process, and Tony admitted that fact and felt humbled by it.

In the process of his transformation, he met women who, five years before, would have turned their noses up at his offer to clean their toilets. None knew he'd been a street rat, as he'd been called on several occasions. They never saw past the charm, the polish. They never saw the kid who had eaten out of garbage Dumpsters when he'd been hungry enough. They saw Antonio Viscolli, a man with money, power, connections, and a bit of danger lurking in the background behind those dark brown eyes.

Tony enjoyed women, enjoyed being with them, enjoyed entertaining them. He had scores of women across the country he could call on at any time if he wanted a date or a hostess. It had become something so normal to him that he never gave much thought to it. Most didn't even mind the platonic boundaries of their relationships, always hopeful that he might fall in love and propose, giving away the coveted title of Mrs. Antonio Viscolli.

This woman was different. He didn't have a finger on it yet. Something about her, something in her, made her different. His attraction to her had been instant and absolute. Was he listening to God's whispered voice in his ear, or his own human weaknesses, his own longing and loneliness? He didn't know. He just knew that he must see her again. He felt led to get to know her.

Pushing all thoughts out of his mind, he concentrated solely on the rhythm of his strokes. Flexing his arms, he cut the oars through the water, sending the boat sleekly across the surface as a trickle of sweat rolled down his back between his shoulder blades.

That insufferable, miserable—. **Robin's hand** slapped the side of the wall, cutting off the next words in her mind.

Robin stood under the weak spray of the shower,

wishing that the wall she slapped with her open palm could be him. His face. No, she changed her mind. She wouldn't give him a full slap on the face. No, she'd curl her hands until her nails would rake some of the handsome off, until they drew blood and left scars.

The nerve of the man.

She slopped shampoo into her palm and started the long process of washing her hair. How dare he? Leaving her a tip that morning under his plate that nearly matched to the penny the tip put on his account that she and ten others split. Who did he think she was? *What* did he think she was? It seemed like he made it clear what he thought of her, asking what she'd do to keep her job at Hank's a secret from Benedicts'.

Oh, and the way that he just smiled that irritatingly polite smile at her through the rest of breakfast. Plus he had that stupid trick in the way he held her eyes, giving her the feeling that he wanted to be alone with her in a candlelit room, and the whole time giving some stupid speech about the economic development of Boston. He never even tripped on his words, not when she glared at him, nor when she turned her back on him.

She scrubbed her scalp until it hurt, then finally took mercy on her poor roots, knowing she would have to bind the strands tightly in a bun for another grueling eight hours.

She would just put the bills into a little envelope and mail the money right back to him. She didn't need him or his money.

She closed her eyes and rested her cheek against the tile wall. If she could just take a break. "Two more years," she said out loud, then ducked her head back under the spray to finish washing the suds away.

Feeling better after pounding the shower wall some more, she sat at her kitchen table, a tuna sandwich and a cup of coffee at her elbow, and figured out her budget. She'd had a good summer, considering the way business declined at Hank's during the school's off-season. Because, without fail, Benedicts' always had a great summer.

While she had very little money for herself, very little extras, she could pay all of the bills this month without a hitch. She finished balancing her checkbook and found the money that Maxine deposited into her account. She made a note to call the bank and have it transferred. She'd made a vow to do this alone, and she intended to see it through to the end.

Maxine had tried giving her checks, but eventually quit when Robin kept handing them back to her torn up. She had tried cash, but it kept ending up on her bed. Now she'd resorted to directly depositing the money. Robin simply opened her sister a savings account and had the money transferred as soon as she discovered it.

It bothered her that she hadn't been grocery shopping in months. Maxine beat her to it. If she could take the food back, she would. Of course she couldn't, so she simply added what she guessed Maxine spent on the food to the amount that got transferred into the savings account.

Robin popped a peppermint onto her tongue and looked at the balance in the account. She didn't have a whole lot left, but she would have enough from tonight's tips to fill her car up with gas. Then she wouldn't have to worry about anything for another week.

Just as she capped her pen, she heard the apartment door open and close, and watched Sarah come around the corner of the kitchen. She wore a baggy T-shirt that advertised Hank's and a pair of baggy jeans. She stopped short when she saw Robin sitting at the table.

"Hey. I expected you to be sleeping."

Robin shrugged and sucked on her peppermint. "I guess I'm not used to napping." She stared at Sarah while the young woman rummaged in the refrigerator and pulled out salad makings. "How did your test go?"

Sarah groaned as she tore off lettuce leaves and dropped them into a bowl. "Microbiology." She popped a cherry tomato into her mouth and grinned around the fruit. "However, I think I aced it. Whether or not I'll remember anything remains to be seen, but at least I got through the exam."

"That's great." Robin reached across the table and snagged a slice of cucumber from the bowl. "Your dip's in the fridge."

"Thanks, Robin. I appreciate that."

The front door opened and shut again. Seconds later, Maxine footed into the kitchen looking as if dashing toward an unseen finish line. She wore a plum colored skirt and a white silk blouse, and somehow had all of that hair contained in a stylish twist on the back of her head. Robin thought that the contrast between her two sisters was almost comical.

"Hi honey, I'm home. What's for lunch?" she grinned, looking over Sarah's shoulder. She snagged a slice of carrot from the bowl.

"If you two want some of this, I can make a bigger salad," Sarah frowned.

Robin winked at Maxine and snuck a tomato. "Don't be silly. We can just eat off of yours."

Maxine kicked her heels off, pulled out a chair, and sat down. "You have any meat to go with that?"

Sarah shuddered. "Do you know the types of hormones and other toxins they pump farm animals full of? How can you eat that?"

Maxine grinned and snatched a peppermint out of Robin's tin. "Luckily, I studied mundane things like art and drafting, and have no need for that kind knowledge. And after my double cheeseburger on my way home just now, I must say that ignorance is bliss." She turned her head and looked at her older sister. "You look tired."

"Don't I always look tired?" She stood and stretched, then threw the checkbook and calculator into a drawer. "I need to get ready to go to Hank's." She lifted her hair and let it fall. It had nearly dried. "What are you two doing tonight?"

Sarah carefully added extra virgin olive oil and a dash of vinegar to her salad. "I have to take that dip out to my parents'. I'll probably just spend the night there."

Maxine propped her feet on the chair Robin had just vacated and grinned. "I am taking the rest of the day off and treating myself to a mini-spa day. I have a hot date."

"You always have a hot date." Sarah grabbed a fork and sat down. "I don't see how you ever made it through college."

"It was definitely a juggling act." She stood and grabbed a glass out of the drainer on the side of the sink, flicking the faucet handle up to let cool water fill the glass. "I had to work for this one, though. This guy ignored signals for months. I thought I was going to have to get a neon sign." She took a long pull of water as she sat back down.

Robin laughed on her way out of the room. "What? You don't have one?"

Maxine leaned the chair back and stuck her head through the doorway. "You're lucky I already took my shoes off, or I'd be throwing one at you."

The shutting of her bedroom door muffled the sound of Robin's laughter. Maxine sighed and looked at Sarah. "I'm getting worried about her."

Sarah reached behind her, opened the refrigerator door from her seat, and pulled out a bottle of water. "I don't think you have to worry about her. She's strong. Stronger than I could ever hope to be."

Maxine frowned. "I don't know. Every month that passes, she's losing something."

"What are you talking about?"

She shrugged, not really knowing how to word it. She thought about her conversation with Robin the night before. "Her spark for life, maybe."

Sarah stared at her while she chewed. She finally swallowed and slowly licked her lips. "Did she ever have one?"

Maxine looked at a spot above Sarah's shoulder and slowly nodded. "Yeah. It used to be there. It only showed when she wasn't paying attention, but it was definitely there."

"I think she just works too hard. I wish she'd let me take out a student loan or get a job or something. Anything that would help her out."

Maxine snorted. "Good luck trying. I think it's more than that. I can't quite put my finger on it. When I do, I'll figure out what to do."

Sarah pushed her bowl away and leaned forward. "Can I ask you something?"

Maxine shrugged. "Sure."

"Do you remember that night?"

A chill skirted up her spine, and the memory assaulted her. Suddenly, she hid in the back in the dark closet, listening to the footsteps of the man coming closer. She shook it off and focused back on Sarah's face. "Yeah. Why?"

She looked behind her, then back at Maxine. "I don't remember any of it. Not even her. Sometimes, I get little flashes. Why is that? I was nine years old. How can I forget it?"

Memories crammed into the front of Maxine's mind. Normally, she kept them pushed so far back that she could go for days without remembering any of it. Like a slide show, they popped in front of her vision, one at a time. The dingy apartments, the smell of burning drugs, the rotten food, the odorous men. Ugh! So many men constantly coming and going.

She pushed it all away and realized that her hands had started to shake. "Trust me, honey, you don't want to remember."

Robin entered the lobby of Hotel Viscolli Boston. Green marble, elegant brass, high ceilings, starched uniforms, overstated elegance—it all formed together to one impression in her mind. Wealthy power. She swallowed hard, knowing that her black pants and white shirt, her old ugly clunky shoes and her worn canvas backpack made her look like a waif compared to the coifed, tucked, heeled women gracing the lobby. Steeling her shoulders against the aura of intimidation, she crossed the expanse of the marble foyer and found a smiling, uniformed brunette behind the counter.

"May I help you?" She asked with a singsong voice.

On the wall above her head, scrolling brass read: Whatever you do, work at it with all your heart, as working for the Lord, not for men. Colossians 3:23

Robin kept from fidgeting. "I'd like to see Mr. Antonio Viscolli, please."

The woman gestured with her hand. "Mr. Viscolli's offices are on the twentieth floor. The elevators are right around that corner there."

Robin looked to where she pointed, saw the elevator sign, and looked back to her and said, "Thank you."

"You're very welcome," she said with an impossibly large smile. "Have a wonderful day."

Robin lost a little of the confidence she'd stored up to step into the lobby during the elevator ride up. She had almost changed her mind about it when the doors opened. Because a receptionist sitting behind a large half-mooned desk saw her and smiled, Robin felt obligated to step off of the elevator and into the lobby of the office floor. Her feet sank into the lush carpet and her eyes skimmed the leather furniture and black granite tables. While the lobby screamed wealth and power, this floor radiated it like an actual energy source. Robin's stomach clenched.

"Good afternoon. May I help you?" The receptionist asked.

"Yes." It came out a little hoarse, so Robin cleared her dry throat. Her eyes caught the scrolling brass on the wall behind the desk that said: *He has showed you, O man, what is good. And what does the Lord require of you? To act justly and to love mercy and to walk humbly with your God. Micah 6:8.* What was this place? A church or something?

"I'd like to see Mr. Viscolli, please."

"I'm sorry, but Mr. Viscolli is not in right now." She pulled a pink pad close to her and picked up a pen. "May I take your name?"

What could she do now? "Never mind. I'll—"

The woman looked over Robin's shoulder. "Mr. Viscolli!" She said, her voice a surprised gasp.

"Maggie." Robin felt her shoulders tense so tightly that it hurt. She would have recognized that rich, baritone voice without the receptionist's confirmation. "I stopped in the lobby and grabbed a smoothie, so I decided to take the front elevator." Robin turned. He wore shorts and a golf shirt, his tanned legs and muscled arms somehow not looking out of place in the elegant business reception area. "Please hold any—" As their eyes met, his sentence faltered. His forward motion ceased so quickly that some of the drink in his hand threatened to slosh over the side of his cup. He stared at her and his mouth opened and closed once. "I—"

Not waiting for him to demand a reason for her presence there or, worse yet, not recognize her at all, Robin pulled the envelope full of money out of her pocket and slapped it against his chest. "I can't stay. I just wanted to return this."

She let go of it and the envelope fell to the carpet. He still hadn't moved. She ignored it and rushed past him to the elevators, frantically pushing the button and hoping that the car hadn't gone to another floor yet.

"I'm not what you think I am," she said. She looked back at him. He had moved enough to turn and continue staring at her, but the money still lay at his feet. "I never have been and I never will be." Wanting to cry with relief as the door slid open immediately, she stepped into the car and hit the button to take her to the lobby. As the doors closed on his astounded expression, she said, "Never."

While the elevator descended, gliding almost imperceptibly downward, Robin leaned against the mahogany walls and put her hands against her chest. Her heart pounded in her ears. Goodness, but he was a handsome man. Infuriating, but handsome. She closed her eyes and leaned her head back, willing her heart to resume its normal rhythm so that she could catch her breath.

CHAPTER FOUR

Robin cornered Hank in the dry storage room. "What is this?" she asked, waving the schedule for next week in one hand. The corners had torn from where she ripped it off of the bulletin board.

He looked up from his inventory clipboard and peered at the paper. "It would appear to be the schedule for the week beginning tomorrow." He dipped his head down and looked at her over his half-eyes. "Why do you have it all balled up in your hand?"

"Because, once again, I'm not bartending. Last week, you had me waitress, food prep, hostess. This week I'm doing food ordering and working as hostess? I need the tips from bartending, Hank. You know that. What's going on?"

Hank rubbed the back of his neck. "I, ah..." He cleared his throat. "Listen. I need an assistant manager. Marjorie is wanting to be down in Florida more and more, with the kids. The work here, our work here, is really getting in her way of enjoying her grandchildren."

Robin smiled at the thought of Hank's wife, doting on her 'grandbabies' as she called them. "I bet."

He took off his reading glasses and slipped them into his front pocket. "I thought I'd schedule you around the restaurant, give you a feel of all of the other jobs, then offer it to you."

"Offer what to me?"

"The position."

She had nothing to say. "Me?"

Hank inhaled deeply then huffed out the air. "I don't really know how to tell you this. Okay. I'll just spit it out." He moved quickly, put a large hand on her small shoulder. "I love you like one of my own, Robin. You and your sisters. Helping you out, making sure you got custody of Maxi was one of the things I know I did good in my life. You're one of the reasons this restaurant has flourished the way it has, one of the reasons that I can retire and know I made a success out of two careers."

She licked her lips and fought panic. "Retire?"

He nodded. "Retire. We're selling out, heading south to be with the kids."

"Selling out?" Her hand trembled in his, so she pulled it away. "You're leaving me?"

He sighed and sat down on a pallet of flour. "The new owner, he's going to close down the bar. I wanted to get you into the assistant manager position before the transition was final so that you'd be locked in."

Robin paced the small room. "What will happen to us? All of us? We just get dumped?"

"No. It's a condition of the contract. You all stay, benefits and everything."

She whirled around. "Contract? You've already done this?"

"Yesterday."

"Yesterday, as in Friday?" She could hear the hurt in her own voice dripping over every word. She hated showing that weakness. "You didn't even think to tell me?" Robin quickly turned her back and buried her face in her hands. As surreptitiously as possible, dug her fists into her burning eyes. She felt so tired, so very tired. She turned and stared at him. "Sorry. I have to go."

He was off of his perch and in front of the door before she had even turned all the way around. "We'll finish this."

"You've already finished it. You're leaving. You're abandoning me." Her voice trembled.

He put his hands on her shoulders and squeezed. "No, Robin, I'm not. I'm staying on as manager for a couple more years. Besides, you're almost done. Two more years, right? You have this job guaranteed for at least that long." He gave her a small shake. "I didn't think you could do it. I never told you that. You've held out, though, and you've made me proud. As proud as a dad can be for his daughter. But, this is something me and the wife need to do. And when I do leave, I'm leaving you in good hands."

Weary now that the short burst of adrenaline left her, she rested her face on his chest and let his strong arms envelop her. "I'll miss you so much."

He kissed the top of her head and squeezed her tight. "I'll just be waiting for you to take a vacation, come down and visit once Sarah's done."

Her words were muffled against his flannel shirt. "Deal."

Robin always took Sundays off. She knew she had to have at least one day to completely recoup.

She rarely got in from Hank's before two in the morning, and she would fall onto her bed and sleep until at least noon. Eventually, she would make it out of bed, drink a cup of coffee, eat a really big breakfast which Maxine usually prepared, then fall back asleep for a few hours.

Sunday nights she reserved for lounging on the couch, zoning out in front of the television. Sometimes, her sisters persuaded her to go with them to see a movie, but those times came few and far between. She rarely liked to leave the one day she could stay home.

She woke up this Sunday with a horrible headache. It didn't surprise her, considering the fact that sleep evaded her that morning. The last time she'd looked at the clock, the blurry numbers of 6:27 stared back at her. When she rolled back over, 11:13 signaled the end of trying to sleep. Sadness overwhelmed her. Loss of an important part of her life threatened what tiny bit of security she'd managed to build around her over the last seven years.

Hank had never been just her employer. He'd hired her just days after his youngest daughter moved from home, and Robin had easily slid right into her place. Hank's wife, Marjorie, suffering under some severe empty nest syndrome took her under her wing in her own gentle way.

Hank found her in the back alley the day that she received the rejection on her petition to be Maxine's guardian. An eighteen-year-old bartender wasn't a viable candidate for guardianship of an impressionable young fifteen-year-old. That was what the case worker had said.

Of course, Robin had retorted back on the phone to her that the foster father who'd raped her couldn't be considered better, but the case worker had turned deaf ears on her pleas, and had given her a flat no.

He'd found her with the letter crumpled in her fist, shaking with rage in the back alley. No tears fell from her eyes, but her throat hurt with the need to sob and her eyes burned as he'd sat across from her on a shipping crate and listened to her story. She told him the whole sordid tale. She lay her entire life out for the first time ever. It sounded tragic to her own ears, and after he silently listened to every word, his large hands curled into fists and a muscle ticked in his jaw where he clenched his teeth.

Not long after that, Hank had pulled strings. Retiring so high up in the chain of command in the Navy gave him high strings to pull. He wrote letters to the social services, ensuring that Robin would only work shifts that correlated with school hours as long as Maxine was a minor, and ensured that his own wife would watch over her in the summer months. He made telephone calls, took people to lunch, and—Robin was sure—issued a few veiled threats, until the day Maxine sat in her apartment, finally in a safe, permanent home.

Hank made it happen. Without him, Robin didn't know where her fragile family would be. She loved him only second to her sisters and knew that she would lose a part of herself when he left.

She'd never really cried in her adult life; couldn't remember the last time a genuine tear had fallen from her eyes. She had experienced so much in her life that she feared if she started crying about it all, she would never stop. Still, the back of her throat ached as she lay in her bed and stared at the ceiling.

Silence hung over the apartment like a cloak. Sarah was likely at church and Maxine must be off somewhere. She didn't even have anyone to complain to or whine to, and that seemed to make it worse.

She groaned and rolled out of bed. Hank's didn't open until four on Sundays, but he would be there. He usually worked on paperwork on Sundays. Maybe she could talk him into making her lunch, let them have an afternoon like they used to have before she started putting sisters through college.

If the chill last night gave any indication, the Indian summer had ended Fall definitely arrived, putting a crispness in the air, so she dressed to suit the weather. She noticed as she buttoned her jeans that she'd lost some more weight, but simply shrugged it off and secured the pants with a leather belt. She added a white T-shirt, a green and blue flannel shirt, and a pair of hiking boots, and left the apartment within fifteen minutes.

She lived close enough to Hank's to walk it. The early afternoon air crisply stung her cheeks, but her eyes watered against the bright sun shining against the deep blue sky. As she inhaled the cool air and slipped a pair of sunglasses on her nose, she decided that just being outside in the daylight without deadlines or appointments lifted her spirits.

She recognized Hank's car, but she didn't pay attention to the other two there. They could have belonged to patrons who'd been too intoxicated to make their way home the night before. They could have belonged to people from the city who had headed to their little corner for antique shopping. Either way, she was unprepared for anyone else to be in the building when she walked inside.

She stepped through the entrance and stood just inside, slipping off her sunglasses so that her eyes could pan the room. She stood near the hostess stand and looked around. Marjorie had done an amazing job decorating the interior of Hank's. The Spanish tile floor created a stunning terracotta and beige pattern through the rooms. Black tablecloths covered square tables, and charcoal drawings of turn-of-the-century Boston covered the beige walls. Off to her right and through double frosted glass doors sat her former territory. The bar acted as its own entity. It sat off of the path of the main restaurant. The doors stood closed now, and Robin went in that direction, wanting to take a long look before the new owners took it away.

Twenty black leather barstools surrounded the large circular bar. Ten small circular tables sat around the rest of the room, providing a place for two or three people to perch on high chairs or stand while waiting for a table. Two large flat screen televisions adorned the small room, one always turned to a sports station and the other always on a 24-hour news station but on mute with closed captioning enabled. The opposite side of the room had access to the patio area, and on warm summer days, half of the wall would slide out and a tiki-bar could be set up to serve drinks and appetizers.

Never again would a warm summer breeze blow on her while she made frozen drinks and laughed with college students enjoying the relaxed summer schedule. Never again would another football season crowd so thick force her waitresses to access her through the kitchen door. Seven years of seasons coming and going suddenly ended. What now?

Tony Viscolli came through the kitchen door and saw

her, staring at the patio doors with a mournful expression on her face. He took the opportunity to silently observe her, knowing she would tense up as soon as she saw him.

She'd worn her hair down today. It fell long down her back almost to her waist. It shined around her head, a glowing, cascading mass that fell halfway down her back. He almost chuckled aloud at the romantic description, but anything else seemed too tame. He wanted to feel it entwine itself around his fingers.

He must have completely lost his mind.

He'd seen her several times over the past two weeks, at Benedicts' and at the bar, and while he made it a point to ensure she did not serve him, he also made it a point to be where he could watch her.

She'd given him his tip money back, every dime. With his confused receptionist watching, he'd observed the elevator doors close on Robin then laughed out loud. If he didn't already feel intrigued to the point of obsession, that would certainly have triggered it.

While he'd contemplated the notion of having her researched several times over the last two weeks, he decided against it. He definitely had the resources, but he decided that he would learn what made her tick the old-fashioned way.

When she walked farther into the room, far enough away from the door to prohibit a quick exit, he finally decided he ought to make his presence known. He stepped forward and pretended to cough.

She turned toward the sound, and he watched her face the very second recognition dawned in those blue, blue eyes. Sapphires. She needed a band of sapphires around her neck, encased in platinum.

"You!" As their eyes clashed, her face hardened and she froze. "What are you doing here?"

His eyebrow quirked upward. His lips barely twisted into a sardonic grin. "I could ask you the same question."

"That's none of your business."

"Oh," he said, opening the small refrigerator under the bar and pulling out a tonic water. "I disagree."

She surged forward and slapped her palm on the top of the bar. "You can't be back there." She watched as he reached above his head and pulled down two glasses. "What are you doing? Get away from there."

He poured half of the bottle into one glass and the other half into another. "Here. Have one."

He stayed behind the bar, thinking he should keep something immobile between them. It kept her from scratching his eyes out, and it kept him from touching her.

She was furious.

And magnificent.

"Don't make me call the police, Mr. Viscolli."

He chuckled and watched her teeth clench in anger. "And what would you say the charges should be, Robin?"

"Trespassing, theft. I'm sure there's more. Did you break in?"

He took a long swallow of his drink, a diamond winking on his little finger. "Sorry. None of those charges would stick."

She moved behind the bar and snatched the glass from his hand. She dumped both glasses out in the sink and turned the water on. "I wouldn't be so sure," she snapped.

"Oh, I am. You can't trespass on your own property."

The glasses clattered into the sink, forgotten. She

turned and stared at him with wide, almost panicked eyes. "Your property?"

He stepped forward and reached behind her. She took a quick step back, then color flooded her face when he simply turned off the water at the sink. He stood close enough now that he could smell her perfume. "Signed and sealed. They might haul you away for trespassing, of course."

"No," she said. Her eyes darted to the left and right. "Where's Hank?"

He inclined his head toward the kitchen, and she turned and ran without a backward glance.

Robin slammed the kitchen doors open and immediately spotted Hank at the stove. "Do you have any idea what you've just done?"

He turned at the sound of her voice and grinned the second he saw her. "Robin! Come in, come in." He had a spatula in his hand and waved it toward the stainless steel counter. "Barry Anderson, Robin Bartlett." He smiled at her and turned back to the stove. "You're in time to eat one of my burgers."

She looked at the guy sitting at the counter without actually seeing him. "Hi," she said distractedly, then immediately rounded back on Hank. "Do you have any idea who you just sold your place to?"

With an expert flick of his wrist, he turned the frying meat over on the grill. "Sure. Tony Viscolli. Nice kid. I like him."

"He isn't nice and he isn't a kid."

"You'll like him once you get to know him." He moved to the wall and opened the oven to check on something in there, then shut the door before he turned and winked at her. "He comes across a little hard at first, but then you get to know him."

"Hank," she started, then remembered she had an audience. Then she didn't care that she had an audience. "Hank, I've served him at Benedicts'."

He whistled under his breath while he set rolls out on the counter. "I forget sometimes that you know several of the more prominent people in the city."

She wanted to scream. "Hank, listen to me. You can't sell your place to him."

Her tone suddenly reached him, and he stopped all movement and looked full at her. "What are you talking about?"

"I'm telling you. I served him at Benedicts'. Hank, he implied that I could be bought."

His expression was blank for a moment before rage overtook it. "What are you talking about?" he bellowed.

She crossed her arms over her chest and lifted her chin. "Just that. He implied he could buy me. You'll just have to tear up the contracts."

"Tony wouldn't do that. You're either mistaken or lying." The man at the counter spoke for the first time, and she whipped her head around to look at him.

"How do you know?"

"Because I know." He rose to his feet and she had to lift her head to keep eye contact. "He wouldn't, and he wouldn't have to."

"He did."

"I seriously doubt it."

She recognized him now. He drank a Shirley Temple one night a couple of weeks ago in the bar. Then she suddenly realized where she'd seen Viscolli that day at Benedicts' when she'd been sure that she'd seen him before. They'd come in together, a Shirley Temple and a ginger ale. "He all but said the words."

"That's not the same as saying them."

Dismissing him, because he clearly acted as Tony's crony, she turned her attention back to Hank. "Listen to me, he—"

"What exactly did he say?" Barry asked.

She sighed, and with an embarrassed flush, she relayed the conversation she'd had with that man.

Hank frowned and looked at Barry then back at Robin. "You could almost read anything into that, Robin."

"You can't read anything into it that isn't there."

Barry interrupted again. "Maybe he was simply flirting."

"Flirting?" She turned and faced him fully. "Mr. Anderson, I've worked at Benedicts' for six years. The men who are members there and who dine there do not flirt with the wait staff. They sleep with them, pay them—or some of them anyway—but there is no casual flirting."

He raised an eyebrow. "In the last six years, have you ever served Antonio Viscolli?"

"Not that I can recall, other than that one time."

"Don't be so quick to lump him into a category, Miss Bartlett. You'll find he doesn't fit."

Snarling at the grease ball's wingman, she turned back to Hank. "Are you not going to pay any attention to what I told you?"

He glared at her. "Don't be insulting, Robin. I heard every word and I'll look into it."

"But—"

"I said I'd look into it."

She let out a breath and nodded. "Okay. Okay, thanks." She turned and looked at the other man, but didn't speak. Then she started toward the back door. "I'm going back home and going back to bed."

CHAPTER FIVE

rowing up, **Tony knew nothing** of boundaries or rules. When he gave his life to the Lord, he made a personal vow to always play by the rules. Usually, he did. In this case, though, he felt he had to cross a few boundaries—not necessarily break rules, but just toe a line -- or two. Today those boundaries included looking through personnel files until he obtained a certain home address.

He climbed the threadbare stairs to the third floor, walked down the long hallway, and scanned the apartment numbers on the doors until he came to the one he sought. He paused, took a deep breath and rapped on the door with his bare knuckles.

He expected Robin to open the door, take one look at him, and snarl. To his surprise, when the door swung open, he came face to face with one of the most beautiful women he'd ever seen. She stood nearly as tall as he, with long straight black hair, almond shaped eyes, and dark skin. She was obviously of Native American descent, but her green eyes told a story of mixed blood.

"May I help you?" she asked over the rock music pounding out of the stereo from somewhere in the apartment.

Giving her his warmest smile, he slipped his hands into his pockets and rocked back on his heels. "I'm looking for Robin."

"Robin?" She raised an eyebrow. "Really?"

"Robin Bartlett. She does live here, doesn't she?"

She grinned at him while she crossed her arms over her chest and leaned against the door frame. "My sister Robin? A man is here to see my sister Robin?"

He found it impossible not to return her smile. "I would hope that's what I am."

She laughed and straightened. "Please, come in. If you're a psycho with a knife, just don't sneak up behind me. I really hate that." She gestured inside and stepped out of his way as he came in. "I'm Maxine. Call me Maxi."

"Tony."

She waved a hand toward a worn couch as she flipped off the stereo. "Have a seat. I have no idea where she went or when she'll be back, but I'm guessing it will be soon. It's Sunday, and she's always home on Sundays."

He nodded as he sat on the couch and relaxed against the cushions. "Actually, I saw her not twenty minutes ago."

Maxine raised an eyebrow. Tony could tell she wanted to ask questions, but refrained. "Can I offer you anything to drink, Tony?"

"No, thanks." He leaned forward with his knees on his elbows. "I should warn you, though. Robin won't exactly be excited to see me."

Maxine's face lit up with a huge grin. "Oh, this is too good," she said. Still smiling, she gestured at her outfit of shorts and an oversized sweatshirt. "Excuse me while I change into something more appropriate for company." Her voice carried to him as she walked down the hallway. "This is just too good."

He stayed where she had seated him, but inspected the room in her absence. It could have fit into his closet, he thought, wondering how two girls lived together in such a small space. Somehow, they had squeezed a couch, an overstuffed chair, and a scarred coffee table into the tiny room. Crammed into the corner sat a small television. A bar separated the kitchen from the living room. The kitchen looked just big enough to have the smallest of tables in it. One person would be cramped living here for any length of time.

Seconds later, Maxine returned, still in the sweatshirt, but now wearing a pair of jeans. "So, what brings you here today, Tony?"

He toyed with the ring on his finger. "I thought I'd try to convince your sister to celebrate my birthday with me tonight." He glanced at her. "Think I could talk her into it?"

Throwing herself onto the couch opposite him, she curled her legs underneath her and grinned. "You say you don't think she'll really appreciate you coming by?"

"Yes, though that may be an understatement."

She chuckled. "Oh, this will be good."

He cut her a look from the corner of his eyes. "You keep saying that."

She reached out with a long arm and playfully poked his shoulder. "Are you sure you're not an axe murderer or a bill collector?"

He frowned. "I'm afraid not. Why do you ask?"

"Because you may wish you had some kind of weapon before it's all said and done." She looked at her watch. "If she's not back by two, I'm going to have to call and cancel a date. I can't miss this."

Remembering the spark in Robin's eyes the last time she looked at him, Tony smiled.

Both heads turned expectantly as the door opened, and Tony watched a woman walk in with a small enough frame that she could easily pass for a child. She had curly, curly brown hair and an almost porcelain complexion. She made him think of a pixie.

"Hello," she said in a soft voice, staring at him with large hazel eyes set behind a pair of wire framed glasses. "Are you Dwayne?"

Maxine laughed. "No, he's not coming until two." Maxine gestured between the two. "Sarah, Tony. Tony, my sister Sarah." She grinned at her sister. "Sarah, Tony's here to see Robin."

Sarah's eyes widened and she slowly lowered herself into the chair. "Robin? Really?" She looked at Tony again, a closer inspection, and the wonder on her face grew. "Our Robin? Goodness."

Tony began to question whether coming here had been a wise decision. He shifted uncomfortably and leaned forward, putting his elbows on his knees. "Maybe I should just come back another time."

Maxine sprang to her feet. "No. No, don't do that." She looked at her sister and back at Tony. "We're not trying to make you uncomfortable. I apologize. We're just surprised, that's all."

"Why?"

Maxine shoved her hands in her pockets and ran her tongue over her teeth. "Well…" The door opened, cutting off her next words.

Tony felt a little excitement of anticipation skirt along his spine. This time Robin entered, carrying a grocery sack, her face flushed from the bite of Fall in the air. "You aren't going to believe this," she said. She had her back to them, securing the locks on the door as she spoke. "I was just at Hank's…"

She turned around and froze. Her eyes darted from Tony to Maxine to Sarah and back to Tony. "Oh, you have got to be kidding me!"

He smoothly made it to his feet. "Hello, Robin."

She bared her teeth at him. "You're like a bad penny. No. A bad dream." She stormed toward the kitchen. "A nightmare."

Wondering about the wisdom of the act, especially considering the innumerable weapons that could be found in a standard kitchen, he followed her. He leaned against the doorway and watched her slam the bag of groceries onto the top of a small table. He watched her open and shut cupboards nearly hard enough to break them off at the hinges as she put the items away. The whole time she muttered under her breath.

He flinched a little at her colorful language before he spoke. "I talked to Hank right after you left."

She whirled around, surprised to see him right there. "Did I ask?"

He continued as though she had. "I feel it is important for us to clear the air."

The grocery bag empty, she crossed her arms over her chest and leaned against the stove, snarling at him. "So you invade my house and consume my personal time? If you want to clear the air, you can do it during my working hours."

He straightened and came all the way into the room, filling up the small space, stopping just a few feet from her. "This has nothing to do with business, Robin. It's all personal."

"Nothing between us is personal."

He moved forward one more step. She visibly stiffened. "I think that there is a very serious misunderstanding between us that needs to be cleared up right away."

She tilted her chin up, almost looked down her nose at him. He had to bite the inside of his lip to keep from grinning. "Are you talking about your implication that I could be bought?"

He held up a finger. "See? There it is. I never implied that."

"Ha!" She straightened and threw her hair over her shoulder. "Now you're a liar and a jerk. Wow. All of the things I thought about you are panning out to be true. They say one should never judge by first impressions alone." His narrowed his eyes, feeling her intended insult. She clearly realized she had crossed the line when she sighed warily and simply said. "Go away."

"At what point did I imply that you would be willing to trade sex for money?"

She stepped forward and put her hands on her hips. He didn't think she realized that they stood nearly nose to nose. "You implied it when you said my job was in your hands and then asked me what I'd do to keep it. You acted on it when you left me that tip."

Her eyes had darkened to near indigo, and they sizzled with anger. He resisted every urge inside him that screamed to touch her, to soothe her. "That tip wasn't payment to get you into my bed."

"No?" She raised an eyebrow. "Was its purpose not to make me remember you, to fawn after you, to perhaps flirt back the next time you happened to be seated at a table I serve?"

He saw where she led the conversation and grinned. "Yeah."

"Then I would be flattered that the oh so rich Antonio Viscolli actually showed an interest in little dirt poor me, and then I would perhaps jump at the opportunity for a date with you, which would, I'm sure, be scheduled out to end up with us having sex."

He couldn't take it anymore. Just one touch, whether or not he lost the finger. He reached out and found a strand of her hair, letting it wind its way around his finger. "It isn't quite as cut and dry as that, Robin."

He kept his voice quiet, letting it vibrate around her. Her eyes flared and she jerkily looked around, as if seeking an exit. "Please don't touch me."

The panic in her eyes had him back off more than her words. He let go of her hair and stepped away. Without a word to him, she pushed past him and stormed out of the kitchen. Maxine and Sarah didn't even hide the fact that they had stood at the bar, listening to the entire conversation. "I'm going to bed," she told them through gritted teeth. She stopped just before her bedroom door and threw over her shoulder, "Alone."

Sarah and Maxine cringed at the sound of the bedroom door slamming, but Tony leaned against the bar on the kitchen side. "Well," he said, "that went better than I'd anticipated."

Sarah looked at him with her mouth open. "Are you out of your mind? What was it that went so well?"

"Well," he breathed between clenched teeth, "I'm not bleeding, I still have all of my operating parts, and my voice isn't ten octaves higher."

Maxine started laughing, laughing so hard she had to sit on an arm of the chair. She laughed until tears ran down her face, then slowly straightened and wiped her eyes. Tony couldn't help smiling in return. "Oh, I like you. Can I keep you?"

Sarah looked between the two of them and shook her head. "Maybe you should leave," she said to Tony. "I don't know you and I don't think that Robin wants you here."

Maxine stood up and brushed Sarah off with the wave of her hand. "Don't be ridiculous. It's his birthday. We must celebrate."

"Maxine," Sarah said under her breath. "Robin…"

"… needs this." She rounded the corner to the kitchen and elbowed Tony out of her way. "Move over. I'm going to bake you a cake."

"You're going to bake me a cake?" He stared at her in disbelief.

"Sure." She turned her head and looked at her sister, who stared at them both with a mixture of fear and excitement. "And Sarah's going to go to the store and buy the makings of a birthday feast."

Sarah took a step back and held up her hands as if to

ward her off. "No way. I'm not having any part in this."

She dug through a drawer until she came up with a pen and a pad of paper. "Actually, Tony may need to go with you. I'm not going to trust you not to come back with tofu or sprouts or soy milk or some other inedible oddity."

She quickly wrote out a list then grabbed her purse off of the kitchen table. "Just around the corner is a little market. It should have everything you need, so you won't even have to drive." She pulled out her wallet and counted out some money. "Here. This should be enough."

He just looked at the money then back at her, feeling out of control of the situation for the first time in fifteen years. "Really, you don't have to do this."

"Don't be ridiculous. I think it's great." Since he didn't move, she picked up his hand and slapped the list and the money into his palm. "It's about time things got shaken up a bit around here."

He stared down at their joined hands. He could still smell Robin all around him and suddenly thought that it was all a great idea. "Okay, but you don't need to give me any money. I can handle it."

"No one's buying their own dinner on their own birthday when I'm around." She turned him around and pushed between his shoulder blades. "Go on. I'll see you two back in a bit."

"Maxine," Sarah said. She still stood in the same position. "I'm not having anything to do with this."

Maxine grinned at her while Tony held the door open, waiting. "Sure you are. You have to show him where the shop is. Don't be rude to our guest, Sarah."

Sarah tried to stare her down, but Tony watched as she fidgeted with her glasses then let out an uncomfortable breath. "I will accept no responsibility."

Maxine smiled. "What a surprise."

"When it all hits the fan, none of it is going to come back and hit me." She stepped out the door and turned around. "You hear me, Maxi?"

Maxine laughed and shut the door behind them.

She dreamt of him, in a very surreal, very light dream. They stood on the banks of a river, dressed in white. The warm sun shone down from a bright blue sky, and the softly blowing breeze caught the hem of her dress, slowly moving it around her bare legs.

He wore white trousers and a white top, making his skin seem darker, his teeth whiter. They laughed and danced on the grass while butterflies fluttered around them. Then his eyes grew serious and his lips touched hers.

Lost in each other, they fell onto the blanket that suddenly appeared on the grass at their feet. His mouth felt gentle, loving, glorious. Her hands moved in lazy patterns across his back, feeling the hard muscles, loving his strength. He raised his head and smiled down at her, and she saw the need inside her reflected in his eyes.

Then his eyes changed. They became light blue, glassy, red-rimmed. The face lightened, widened, hardened, until she stared at HIM. The bank of the river disappeared, the grass faded, the air chilled. Suddenly, she was in her bed. The single bed with the lumpy mattress and dirty sheets.

A hand covered her mouth, forcing her to breathe through her nose, to smell the gin and tobacco on his breath, the stench making her stomach roll.

She started to fight, but he had pinned her legs and arms with his huge body.

"You can't get away this time, little girl," he grunted in her ear.

She screamed, but he muffled the sound with his hand.

"Not a little girl, though, are ya? No, you're a woman. Or you will be, soon as I'm done with you." A hand gripped her breast, squeezed and twisted it until the pain made her vision gray. She realized that her nightgown was gone.

Vomit clawed at her throat. No matter how she resisted, she didn't ever have the strength to fight him off. A single tear rolled out of the corner of her eye while his laughter echoed in her head.

With a strangled cry, Robin clawed her way out of the dream, bolting into a sitting position on the bed. Her whole body quaked in the aftermath. Her hands trembled and her breath came in quick shaky gasps. Sweat poured over her body, and she lifted the damp tendrils of her bangs to wipe her forehead.

Years had gone by since she'd last had the dream. Sometimes, she dreamt through to the bitter end, sometimes she could pull herself out of it in time. It was so much worse if she didn't get out of it in time.

She started to get out of the bed when she heard a noise in the other room. One or both of her sisters were home, so she stayed still, waiting for the effects of the dream to go away. She didn't want to carry the cobwebs of the nightmare out of the room with her.

She drew her legs up and rested her forehead against her knees. Her breathing gradually slowed. Her hands slowly stopped shaking, and the sweat cooled on her body.

Finally feeling normal again, she got out of bed, changed back into jeans and a loose top, and felt that she could face her sisters.

Wonderful smells assailed her nose when she opened her bedroom door. The scent of something spicy and tangy cooking made her stomach rumble in response. Every step toward the living room seemed lighter, and she almost had a smile on her face as she walked the last few steps.

She smelled it first; the underlying smell of expensive cologne. Then she heard him; that deep chuckle that sent a shiver through her spine. Maxine had better have a new boyfriend who wore costly aftershave and acted annoyingly happy all the time. Then she saw him, sitting forward on the couch, a glass of water in his hand. He had his attention on Maxine, and wore that irritatingly irresistible grin on his face again.

"Oh, you've got to be kidding me," she said.

CHAPTER SIX

Tony slowly set his glass down while he mentally prepared himself for the attack. He let his eyes casually take Robin in, noting her hands clenched into fists as they rested on her hips, recognizing the flush of anger as it moved up her neck to her face.

God, he prayed silently, in his mind, *give me wisdom and patience. I feel like You brought her into my life for a purpose. Keep me from reacting or acting in the wrong way. Keep me strong and keep me pure and tell me what I'm supposed to do here. Amen.*

She was magnificent. He wanted nothing more than to see her smile. He wanted to rub the tension away from her face, to hug her in his arms.

He smoothly rose to his feet and walked toward her. Her sisters left his mind. Nothing around him existed except her. He never even paused his advance, his whole focus on her face. Something skittered in her eyes. Dark shadows that leaped at the edges, interfering with the angry sparks that were for him alone. He wanted to make the shadows disappear. He wanted to have the right to ask her about them, but he did have the right. Not yet.

"This is my house," she spat at him, "and I don't want you here."

He grinned. His bold approach worked. Shadows started moving out of her eyes as irritation replaced them. "You aren't the one who invited me." He'd finally reached her and stood inches away. "What is the matter?" he asked her quietly.

Her eyes widened before they narrowed. "You."

He shook his head. "No. Something else." He reached out and put a hand on each shoulder, squeezing gently. She was too thin. She needed to gain some weight. He felt an overwhelming urge to pull her to him, to shield her from the world, to give her everything his considerable empire could offer. Only, he knew the last thing she wanted was his arms around her, so he squeezed her shoulders one more time and stepped back. "Your sister has invited me to dinner."

As he spoke, the timer went off with a loud, "Ding!" in the kitchen.

Robin looked past Tony to Maxine. "My sister?"

"Looks like dinner's ready," Maxine said, hopping up from the couch. "I'll just set it out and we can eat."

"Why did my sister invite you to dinner?"

In the kitchen, Maxine opened the oven door before she spoke. "We're celebrating his birthday."

Robin's mouth opened and closed. "We?" she finally asked. She moved to the entrance of the kitchen.

Maxine winked. "I am." She pulled a pan out of the oven and set it on the small stove. As she took the oven mitts off her hands, she turned and faced Robin. "Oh, by the way, Tony's my guest. You want to eat what I cooked, you'll have to eat with him. You don't like it, leave."

Robin rounded on Sarah. "How much of this was your idea?"

"I had nothing to do with it." Sarah sank into cushions of the couch. "I accept absolutely no responsibility for this."

Maxine leaned over the bar. "Dinner's ready."

Robin jumped as Tony's hand came up and squeezed the back of her neck. "Smells great," he said, giving her neck a reassuring squeeze before inching past her in the doorway.

It bothered her that his touch actually reassured her. She should feel annoyed that he felt like he could touch her at all, and instead, more shadows from the dream fled at his hand on her neck.

She entered the room and jerked her chair out. Maxine had pulled the spare chair out of her bedroom and shifted the table away from the wall so that four chairs would fit around it. Sarah squeezed past them and claimed the spot in the corner against the wall and Maxine sat next to her, closest to the stove. That forced Robin next to Tony, who sat between Sarah and Robin.

As he sat, he held his hands out, palms up. "Do you mind if I bless the meal?"

Sarah, whose parents did things like pray before meals, answered. "Of course. Thank you."

Tony looked at Robin until she, reluctantly, followed Sarah's lead and placed her hand in his. She felt Maxine take her other hand, but could only concentrate on the feel of Tony's palm against her own. She bowed her head and closed her eyes. Soon, the rich tones of his voice flowed over her, and for the first time since her dream, she felt herself relaxing, felt peace edge its way into the corners of her mind.

"Father God, we thank You for this time of new friendship and fellowship. Thank You for Maxine's generous heart that is keeping me from spending this anniversary of my birth alone. Thank You for bringing this family of sisters into my life. Pour out Your blessings into their lives and enrich them, Father. Thank You for my life. Thank You for all of the ways You have brought such joy to my life, including this wonderful meal. Please bless it and bless the hands that made it. In Your precious holy Son's name, Amen."

He let go of Robin's hand after giving it a squeeze. She raised her head and put her hand into her lap, gripping it with the other. What just happened?

Sarah took the lead and picked up the spoon in the dish of potatoes in front of her. "This smells wonderful, Maxi."

Robin had never seen Maxine off balance before and felt intrigued by the way she just blinked before shaking her head and coming out of it. She smiled broadly. "Thank you." She picked up a platter of chicken and handed it over to Tony. "Please eat as much as you want. There is more than plenty."

Robin recovered from the prayer and glared at Tony while he loaded his plate and picked up his fork and dug in. Robin had no appetite, but she put some sparse servings on her plate and pushed food around while she listened, refusing to interact. Instead, she forced the anger toward him back, intentionally remembering the insult so that she didn't fall under the spell that he apparently wove around her sisters' better judgment.

They laughed at every inane thing he said and blushed like students at a junior high dance when he looked at them. Robin remained unaffected, though. She knew his game and could see right through it. She might have been a lowly servant to him, but she'd been dealing with the public for years and knew how to read into unspoken words and body language.

Clearly, he used her sisters, charmed her sisters, to charm her. What if she occasionally let her guard down and he did just that? Then she'd remember, and slam the walls right back up.

The comfort in his touch softened her. It unnerved her. She'd admit it to herself, if to no one else.

She'd spent the first half of her life avoiding men. The types of the male species that her mother brought home were always far from respectable, and most had lived their lives in a glorification of evil. Then they entered the system and had to contend with the foster fathers. Two of them had tried the same things that her mother's boyfriends always had. One managed to get to Maxine before Robin could get to him. She remembered sitting in the cold police station, waiting to find out if they would press charges against her for stabbing him in the back with his own hunting knife.

Boys in high school had paid very little attention to her. She guessed, looking back now with an adult's eyes, that she had intimidated them. When she'd finally been settled into a relatively good home for girls—and while she made excellent grades and learned quickly—by the time she went to an alternative all-girls' school. She had fallen so behind that she finally dropped out.

She'd had to sharpen her defenses even further

working so young as a bartender. The advances from the patrons would just get worse and worse as the nights wore on and they continued to drink. By the time she'd started working at Benedicts', she used a perfected air of disinterest as her defense, leaving the customers who might otherwise have been interested with the first impression not even to make the attempt.

Consequently, at twenty-eight years old, she had absolutely no experience in dealing with men, unless it came in the form of her job, serving them lunch or a drink. She didn't know how to interact with a man—especially a man like Tony—on any level. Then he had to go and comfort her as if wanting nothing in return, right at one of those moments when everything lay bared naked from her dream. Out of nowhere, she wondered how life would change if she had someone next to her shouldering her burden. He made her want something she never wanted before.

She reminded herself that he thought he could buy her, reminded herself that she hated him and wished she had the energy to tell him. Instead, she just sat at her little table that now seemed too small because he occupied a chair, eating food that she knew for certain would taste good if it didn't all seem to turn to sawdust in her mouth, and watching him charm the socks right off of her own flesh and blood.

When Maxine jumped up and whipped a cake out of the refrigerator, she had enough. Not able to take any more, she pushed away from the table. "You'll have to excuse me," she said as sickly sweet as possible, "but I have some things to do."

She refused to meet his eyes, gave Maxine a look that

left no doubt about how she felt about the entire night, and went to her room. Not knowing what else to do that would get her out of there at eight o'clock on a Sunday night, she grabbed her bag of laundry and stormed out of the apartment, slamming the door as hard as she could on her way out.

The empty laundry room helped. She could not fathom acting pleasant or cordial to some other neighbor doing laundry on a Sunday night. The emptiness of the room afforded her the privacy and the opportunity to slam things around, to kick a couple of machines and listen to the satisfying clang of the metal. Only when she had her laundry sorted, loaded into the machines, and starting the wash cycle did she feel like she had calmed down somewhat.

The room would have looked small even without the four washing machines and dryers, so she sat on the small table someone had shoved into a corner. Most of the time, she risked the possible theft of her clothes to wait for the wash upstairs in her own apartment, but she had no desire to go back up there. Instead, she tested the strength of the table, decided it would probably hold her weight, and scooted on top of it.

A day-old newspaper sat on the table, and for lack of anything better to do, she decided to read it. She skimmed headlines and glanced at pictures without actually retaining anything she saw. Instead, of its own volition, her mind drifted back to dinner.

She tried to get a grip back on the anger, but it had faded away. Instead, she remembered the way his hand felt as it held hers during his prayer, the heat of his skin, the strength. Closing her eyes, she thought back and almost completely recaptured the moment.

Could she actually possible to feel so comfortable around a man that she could enjoy feeling her hand in his? Had she truly missed out on something, as Maxine had suggested to her over and over again? Maybe she should listen to her sister. Robin tried but could not come up with anything that had ever felt so comforting as her hand in his.

She knew that not all men behaved or thought like the ones her mother brought home. That didn't motivate her desire not to date. She just simply refused to need a man, and since so many women she worked with and knew fell prey time and time again, allowing men to chew them up and spit out, she really didn't see what she'd been missing.

Except now, Tony filled her thoughts. If the feelings inside of her were normal, she could almost understand the waitresses she worked with continually falling victim to the men in their lives. Maybe she needed to learn about the male-female dynamics. Maybe Maxine had a point.

She certainly had a willing partner. His interest in her centered only around sex, after all. Perhaps she should just go for it. What could it hurt? Unlike some of the desperate waitresses at Benedicts' hoping to score a rich man, she would go into it with open eyes, expecting nothing else out of it. She had a feeling that Mr. Antonio Viscolli preferred it that way. He could teach her the ropes, so to speak, and they could go their separate ways soon after. She guessed he'd finish his part of the deal at Hank's for another week at the most, then he'd hand the reins over to a manager and that little corner of Boston would no longer hold his attention. Having a physical relationship might even make his constant presence during the transition at least endurable.

A week would be enough time. At least it should. Since she didn't really have any practical experience, she would go into it rather blindly.

How to approach him, though? She thought about it while she transferred clothes from the washers to the dryers. She should take a direct approach. He clearly didn't strike her as the type to play games. She ought to act quickly, too. She had his attention now. Who knew what tomorrow would bring.

Tonight. She should catch him before he left. Leaving her clothes, she burst out of the laundry room and took the first flight of stairs two at a time. She hit the first landing and rounded the corner, only to slam right into the chest of the man she rushed upstairs in such a hurry to see.

"Whoa, slow down," he said, gripping her arms to keep her from falling backward down the stairs, "Are you okay?"

"Yeah." She pulled away out of habit and cringed inwardly at the brief flash of resignation in his eyes. "You're leaving?"

The corner of his mouth tilted up in a mocking smile. "Yes. Please, though. There's no need to beg me to stay. I can't be swayed."

Oh, no. The sarcasm dripped from his words. Maybe she had acted too late. "Um, listen, could I talk to you for a minute?"

Tony's eyebrow rose a fraction of an inch. "Of course." He turned his body slightly, as if to go back up the stairs, but stopped when she put a hesitant hand on his arm.

"No, not up there. I kind of wanted to discuss something, uh, private." She turned started walking down. "We can just talk in the laundry room if you don't mind.

My clothes are almost dry, and if I leave them in there, I risk someone throwing them on the floor."

Tony couldn't help but feel intrigued. Without a second thought, he followed her until they reached a little room on the first floor crammed with machines older than him. Something on the chipped tile floor stuck to the bottom of his shoes, but it was so dingy gray that he could not identify the source. Only one fluorescent light out of three burned, casting the room in weird shadows. Layers of advertisements covered the bulletin board.

Robin turned to face him as soon as they entered the room and stood there with her hands shoved into the pockets of her jeans while she rocked back and forth on the soles of her feet. "I guess I didn't really plan how I wanted to say this," she said. He thought that maybe her face reddened, but with the low light, he couldn't really tell.

"Saying something outright usually works," he said. She'd been civil to him for about fifty-seven seconds. He wondered if he should begin to worry.

She huffed out a breath and looked over his shoulder. "I want to sleep with you."

He didn't know for sure how long it took for the words to sink in. He knew he stared at her, speechless, for several seconds, and managed to remember to close his mouth before he looked like an idiot. After it all clicked in and made sense, once he found his tongue again, he could speak. "Excuse me?"

She met his eyes this time. Nothing reflected out of the blue depths that would make him think this was one big joke. "I said, I want to sleep with you."

"Okay. That's what I thought you said." Did he pinch himself now in order to wake up from this odd daydream, or wait for this to play itself out? "May I ask why?"

Her shutters came back into place. He could almost hear them slamming shut. "Look, never mind. Maybe this wasn't a good idea."

She would have brushed by him if he hadn't grabbed her arm. "Nope. You started this. See it through. You couldn't stand the sight of me an hour ago. Why the sudden change of heart?"

Not knowing what to say to that, she decided once again to just take the direct path. "I've never dated anyone before."

She said nothing else. He waited a beat, then two, before prompting her. "Never?"

"Never."

"Why?"

She closed her eyes and let out a breath. "I don't know. I guess…" She opened her eyes and stared into his. He found that he suddenly cared very much about her answer. He cared about what she would say next. "Listen. I had a pretty rough childhood. My mom…" She broke off and looked at her shoes. "Anyway, when I was fifteen we were on our own and bouncing from home to home and eventually I ended up in a girls' home. After that, I had Maxi to take care of and I've just never had the time or inclination to date."

With nervous energy, she paced the tiny confines of the room before she whirled back around. "Look, you can either say yes or no. I'm not holding a gun to your head or anything. I just figured, you know, you want sex and I want to learn about all that." She stopped and looked at him, obviously floundering for something else to say. "Anyway…"

Tony crossed his arms and leaned against a washing machine. "Back up a second. You want me to teach you about sex?"

"Yeah, um, that would be the point."

"I see." He cleared his throat. *Lord, help me,* he thought. He found himself in a bit of a precarious situation, but he didn't want her to stop talking to him, so he played it out. "Why did you pick me?"

She brushed her hair off her forehead in a nervous movement. "Well, you're obviously willing. Plus I figure that you won't be expecting a lifelong commitment or anything, you know? Just some sex, hopefully pleasant if not good, and then you'll be done with Hank's and done with me."

He lost all feeling in his legs and struggled to keep breathing normally. If he hadn't been leaning against the machine, he would have fallen down as he realized the monumental truth.

Dear God, he was in love with her. He always hoped he'd fall in love. He had prayed God would reveal his true love to him one day. As soon as the realization hit, he knew that he'd known it this whole time.

Suddenly spurred with energy, he straightened and stepped forward. "You aren't planning on hiding a knife and plotting a sneak attack or anything, are you? This isn't a tactic to lower my guard, is it?"

Robin huffed out a breath. "You know what? Forget it. This was a bad idea to think of, much less approach you with." With the loud buzz of the dryer, she visibly jumped, then grabbed her laundry bag and started shoving it full of warm clothes. "Let's just pretend this conversation never happened."

He waited until she straightened and turned before stepping forward. As she slung the laundry bag over her shoulder, he reached forward and cupped her cheeks, his fingers splaying down along her neck. He heard the laundry bag land somewhere behind her as she sighed and closed her eyes.

He wondered if she realized that a single tear had escaped out of the corner of her eye and trailed over his thumb. It burned a path across his skin until he feared it would leave a mark. He rubbed his thumbs along the shadows under her eyes. A feeling of tenderness blended with the love that overflowed his heart. He cleared his throat, worried his voice had fled. "You're on."

He felt his neck muscles tense just before she opened her eyes. "Excuse me?"

"I said you're on. I'll teach you. All of it."

She gave a small shake of her head to clear it. "All of it?"

"You said that I wanted sex and that you wanted to learn about all of that. I'm going to teach you about all of that."

Her eyebrows drew together in confusion. "What does that mean?"

"You'll see." He released her face and stepped back while he looked at his watch. "What are you doing tomorrow?"

She rubbed her face with both hands and took a step back away. "Um, the week begins. I have to be at Benedicts' from ten-thirty until three, then Hank's at six to one."

He mentally made all of the arrangements he needed for his schedule and nodded. "Okay. I'll see you tomorrow." He put a hand on either side of her face and kissed her forehead.

CHAPTER SEVEN

obin's car shuddered as she pulled into her parking space and shut it off. As she opened the door, the smell of exhaust stung her nose. It had rolled brand new off of the assembly line about a month before Sarah's birth. As Robin rounded the hood she gave the old girl a little pat, hoping that kindness would make it run one more day.

Just as she stepped onto the curb to go into the building, a sleek red sports car whipped into the spot next to hers. She started to smile, bit her lip, then thought better of it and allowed the smile. As Tony climbed out of the low car, her stomach did a nervous lurch.

He wore a brown leather jacket over a button-down shirt with no tie and a pair of khaki pants. He looked like a model showing off the perfect weekday casual look. He slipped off his sunglasses and smiled as he strolled up to her. "Good afternoon," he said.

Robin's mouth went dry. All day long she could think of nothing but the conversation the night before. She felt some excitement at the prospect of what she proposed, but in the light of day, she also felt quite foolish. "Tony, hi. Look—"

He cupped her elbow under his hand and steered her toward the building. "No time. Go get changed. Jeans are fine. Grab your clothes for Hank's and meet me back down here. We need to drive away fifteen minutes from now."

As he propelled her toward the door, she tried to catch up to what he said. "Leave? What?"

He smiled. "Just get changed. Fifteen minutes." He looked at his watch. "Fourteen."

Flustered, Robin went inside and up to her apartment. She couldn't imagine where he thought they were going when she had a shift start at work in less than three hours, but she followed his instructions until, three minutes later, she locked the door behind her wearing jeans with a cotton top and carrying her Hank's Place uniform in a grocery bag.

She found him where she left him, leaning against the hood of his car, his legs crossed in front of him at the ankle. When he saw her approaching, he straightened and grinned. "Thank you for hurrying," he said, hitting a button on the keys in his hand to release the latch that kept the trunk closed. He took the bag from her and set it in the trunk, then moved to the passenger door and opened it. "We have to be downtown by four."

"Why?" She lowered herself into the car. He shut the door and rushed around the front to the driver's side.

He slid in and started the car in one movement. "Because the movie starts at four."

"Movie? Tony, I have to be at work at six."

Her shoulders hit the back of the seat as he accelerated

out of the parking lot and turned the zippy little car toward downtown. "Robin, do you think I didn't hear you last night or pay attention to what you said?"

She felt her face surge with heat at some of the things she'd said last night. "Of course not."

"Then relax. I know what time you have to be at work." He shot her a glance and reached out, capturing her hand with his. "Have fun without worrying about something."

Instead of arguing about the fact that she didn't worry, when she exactly how much and how often she did in fact worry, she sat back and enjoyed the way he drove the car. Tony had no fear, had amazing confidence, and it came out in his driving. He zipped through the heavy afternoon traffic without stressing out about the way cab drivers cut people off, about missing a green light. He stayed lighthearted, happy, calm, all the while driving with a skill that leant no doubt that he knew exactly how to drive that powerful machine the way the designers intended someone to drive it.

"How was your day?" He asked while idling at a red light.

Robin turned from looking at the downtown scenery around her and found him looking directly at her. "My day?"

His smile made her heart skip a beat. "Yeah," he drawled, "your day. Tell me about it."

"I served brunch and lunch to some power players and some over indulged wives all morning and afternoon."

He put the car in gear and shot away from the light, changing lanes to get around a bus. "Nothing exciting or interesting happened?"

"What? You want me to tell you who had a two-martini lunch?"

She felt her body moving forward against the seat belt as he had to quickly hit the brakes for a cab that jolted out in front of them. "No, Robin. I want to know about YOUR day." He shot her a quick smile. "How about I start? I'll tell you about my day. I was so excited about this afternoon that I forgot about a big meeting. I walked into my office and Margaret, my secretary, told me they were waiting for me in the conference room. I said, 'Who is waiting?' She looked so worried about me that I wanted to hug her."

He stopped talking so she assumed he wanted her to speak. She searched her mind, trying to come up with something interesting to tell him. "After lunch today, when the restaurant was closed, a woman and her daughter came in. They're having her bridal shower there and wanted to discuss menus and staff. They started arguing over what kind of sandwich to serve, and the daughter started screeching at the mom over having chives or no chives in their cucumber sandwiches. She had a total breakdown, and as soon as the mother agreed with her, she immediately calmed down and went on with the meeting." Robin reached up and started pulling pins from her hair. "She made me think of a two-year-old having a temper tantrum."

At another stoplight, Tony looked at her again and forgot what he intended to say as he watched her hair tumble out of the tight bun that had confined it all day. Robin closed her eyes and ran her fingers over her scalp, making Tony wish he were the one doing that. He looked back to the road in front of him in time to see the light change to green. "I imagine you see a lot of temper tantrums there."

"People are people. I like most of my customers."

"You don't mind the excessive lifestyle?"

With a smile, she said, "What do I know of excess? I know of some lifestyles I wouldn't wish on my worst enemies. What I see at Benedicts' is just another way of life."

"You don't wish it were you?"

Now she snorted. "Yeah, right. Because I'd fit in as well as a square peg." She turned her body as much as her seat belt would allow. "I don't care about stuff like that. You can't imagine how good my life is compared to what it used to be. I work hard. I work honest. My sisters are taken care of. That's the only thing that matters to me."

They reached their destination and Tony found a parking space. The ways he could carry that conversation could take hours, could go deep, could go life-altering. Right now, he just wanted to enjoy the next hour or so.

When he pulled into the parking lot of the Museum of Science, Robin felt her eyebrows come together in confusion. Tony tapped the clock on the dash before he turned the car off. "Ten minutes to spare," he said with a wink.

He was out of the car in a fluid movement and had her door open before she even had her seat belt off. He took her hand and helped her out of the car, but instead of releasing her, he just shifted her hand to his other and walked with her to the museum entrance.

"What are we doing here?" She asked.

He gave her hand a squeeze as he opened the door for

her. "Going to the movie. I told you." At the admissions desk, he bought two tickets to the IMAX theater and steered her past the café, the store, and to the theater. There he bought a huge tub of popcorn, a box of chocolate covered raisins, and two drinks. Robin smiled as he flirted with the teenager behind the counter and realized that the tension was gone from her shoulders and neck and she felt lighthearted, almost carefree.

Tony turned to hand over her drink and caught her eyes. He stared at her for a moment, then winked and picked up the rest of the goodies. "Shall we?"

They watched a space documentary presented in 3-D. She sat next to him in a darkened theater on a Monday afternoon, two hours before a work shift started, eating buttered popcorn and chocolate covered raisins, and watching a 3-D movie. Her first experience with a 3-D movie, even, which made her duck the first few times a roving comet or an exploding star headed in her direction.

Some time after he set the empty tub at their feet, Tony took Robin's hand in his. She threaded her fingers with his and settled herself as close as the theater seats would allow and just enjoyed it. Enjoyed herself—enjoyed him—enjoyed sitting next to him.

When the lights came on and the world returned, Robin found herself wishing for just another few minutes. Time wouldn't allow it, especially at rush hour, so they gathered their trash and left the museum.

In the car again, this time headed toward Hank's Place, Tony stopped in the dead-stop traffic and put the engine in neutral. He turned his head and looked at Robin, happy to see the relaxed glow on her face. "Did you enjoy that?"

She smiled as she rolled her head on the seat to look at

him. "That was fun."

"Are you interested in space and the cosmos?"

With a shrug, she turned in her seat so that she nearly faced him. "I don't know. I've never looked into it before." Not wanting him to think she was trying to discourage conversation, she said, "What about you?"

"I am extremely busy." He inched the car forward. "I have very little free time to pursue any intellectual pursuits. However, anything having to do with the majesty of God's creation interests me on a purely emotional level. A friend saw this show with his kids and assured me that it contained nothing that would insult my belief in the Biblical account of creation, so I've been looking forward to seeing it."

She nodded, digesting this new information about him. "You're pretty much unapologetically a Christian, aren't you?"

His laugh surprised her. He shook his head while he grinned and let a minivan in before inching forward some more. "Pretty much," he said with a smile.

"Do you go to church and stuff?"

A break in the traffic allowed him to shoot forward three or four car lengths. "And stuff." When he could take his eyes off the road again, he looked back at her. "If you want to come with me some time, just let me know. I'd love to have you by my side."

What little she knew of church didn't hold any appeal to her. "Uh, thanks, but no thanks."

Tony shrugged and found a spot to surge forward half a block. "It's an open invitation. I reserve the right to ask again."

The next day, Tony showed up outside of Benedicts' in a stretch limo. When Robin climbed in, she saw the picnic he had laid out on the floor of the limo, complete with a red and white checkered tablecloth.

"What is this?" She asked, shedding her coat in the warmth of the interior of the car.

"Well," Tony said, sitting on the floor with his back against the base of the seat. "I wanted to take you on a picnic, but it's so cold outside."

Robin laughed and accepted the bottle of water from him as the limo pulled away from the curb. "You're from Boston, aren't you? You're going to let a little autumn air get in your way?"

He felt a flash of the past for the briefest moment. The shiver that went through him was more than a memory. "I don't do cold." He opened the picnic basket at his side and dug around until he came out with a bowl of grapes. "Soon it will be time for my annual migration to The Keys."

"Florida?" That sounded so far away to someone who had never been outside of the greater Boston area in her life. "What's there?"

He tipped his water bottle toward her as if toasting. "Not cold."

"Ah," Robin said with a wink. "Got you."

Tony held his hand out. "Do you mind if we bless this food before we eat it?"

Robin paused, hesitated, then placed her hand in his. She politely bowed her head but didn't listen much to what he said. Instead, she just listened to his voice, felt the touch of his hand, and wondered. Wondered who this man was who was such a huge financial success, but who wouldn't eat until he'd prayed to God to bless it. What did he think of her, if at all, and her lack of prayer, her lack of God?

Having seen the darker side of the world, of humanity, she wondered how God could even exist. Who let little girls get beaten, starved, terrified, raped? What God would allow that? What kind of God would turn His back on mothers who pumped their bodies full of chemicals and latched on to any man who would take her and her three children in, regardless of the consequence to the daughters?

Maybe Tony didn't know about such darkness, so it gave him an ignorant faith and allowed him to bee-bop from the Keys to Boston and back again without a care in the world. Maybe that's how he could get by with believing what he believed.

He'd said "Amen" and squeezed her hand. She raised her eyes and realized he hadn't released her hand. She sat in the seat and he sat at her feet and held her hand in his, looking at her face. When she finally focused her attention on him, he smiled. "Thank you for sharing this meal with me."

She ran her tongue over her lips in a nervous gesture. "I don't really know what to do next."

He held her eyes for several seconds before letting go of her hand. "You enjoy your meal," he said, handing her a napkin and a bowl with a lid. "When we're done, you will be at Hank's in plenty of time to get ready for work. Maxine packed your uniform for me."

Robin had about five minutes to spare to get dressed. Tony watched her rush through the back entrance to the staff restroom in order to change. He followed more slowly, stopping inside the kitchen door to get a cup of coffee. As he turned, he met Hank's watchful gaze.

Hank stood on the outside of the stainless steel counter, talking to the kitchen staff through the warming lights and to the wait staff who stood around him. He kept talking while he measured Tony, and never one to feel intimidated, Tony returned the stare just as thoughtfully. When Hank finished his predinner rush meeting with the staff, he dismissed them to get back to work and met Tony at the wooden table.

"Robin is like one of my own," he said without preamble.

Tony took a sip of coffee and leaned back against the table. "Glad she has you," he said.

"I'm not going to take a liking to some rich playboy playing games with her."

Tony set his cup on the table behind him and straightened. He reached out and slapped Hank's arm in a masculine sign of agreement. "Neither would I, brother," he said. He looked at his watch. "I have a dinner engagement. Have a good evening."

CHAPTER EIGHT

Robin smiled and headed to the table.

"Hiya."

"Hiya yourself, Casey."

"Alright, then."

After getting a cup of coffee, and with a near groan, she leaned back in the chair and propped her feet in the one across from her. "How's the world treating you?"

"Well, now, here and there, mostly." He lifted a finger to a *sous chef* and leaned under the heating lamps so that she could hear him over the din of the busy kitchen. "You'll be wanting some of my pie to go with that coffee."

"I would, yes." She stifled a yawn as she brought the steaming cup of coffee to her lips.

A uniformed sous chef handed him a platter, which he slid under the lights and nodded at a waitress. She set the hollowed-out bread round filled with steaming chili in front of Robin before returning to wait for her order. "You'll eat that first."

She shook her head. "Really, Casey, I'm not hungry."

"You's looking a bit piqued lately, Robin. You eat that before you get any of my pie." Turning, he put his hands on his skinny hips and barked a few orders to the dinner prep crew.

Feeling a bit like a scolded child, Robin picked up the spoon and took a bite. The spices teased her tongue with just the right amount of heat. Not even thinking about it, she took another bite and another. "Piqued?" she asked with a smile after she had consumed half of the bowl. She broke off a piece of the bread and slowly chewed.

"Ayah. You don't take care of yourself, girlie. Too busy looking after others." He shifted a perfectly fried onion that sat on top of a juicy ribeye and held the plate at arm's length, checking the appearance. Only when it visually pleased him did he slide it to the lingering waiter.

"I take care of myself just fine. I'm just tired. I had to work a breakfast shift this morning on top of the lunch." Now she faced a full Saturday evening and night. She looked down, surprised that she had emptied the bowl. With a contented sigh, she finished her cup of coffee and grinned at Casey as he personally set a slice of pecan pie in front of her.

"You's shouldn't be working two jobs. That girl Maxi is working now, and Sarah's mighty capable of it."

The sweet crunch of the meaty nuts satisfied her tongue too much to form speech right away. Instead, she closed her eyes and enjoyed the flavors. Only after she had swallowed did she open her eyes again, and found a newly refilled cup of coffee in front of her and Casey sitting across from her. "You only sound like Hank when he's not around, Casey. Will I look forward to nightly lectures when he's gone full time?"

He threw his head back and cackled while he slapped his knee. He laughed for about fifteen seconds, then he stopped, shook his head, and abruptly stood and bustled back over to his command perch. "Just take care of yah-self, missy. Kinda like having you around."

She pushed the half-eaten pie away and stood to get ready for work. "Two more years. Then I can slow down." She considered the date and performed a quick mental calculation. "No, wait, not even. This semester's half over by now."

Noise from the bar section of the restaurant invaded the room as the connecting door swung open. Assuming one of the other bartenders came in to gather supplies before the dinner rush began, Robin ignored it until Casey spoke. "You'll be wanting something to eat this early, Mr. V?"

She turned her head and prepared herself for the skip of her heart that suddenly started occurring whenever Tony walked into a room. "No thanks, Casey I'll just grab a coffee."

He strode across the room with a liquid grace a man shouldn't have, squeezing her shoulder as he walked by. With a sigh, she sat back down as he fixed himself a cup of coffee and lowered himself into the chair across from her.

Robin didn't think she'd ever get used to looking at him. She thought after seeing him every single day for a week that she might possibly become immune to his looks, but his handsome face made her heart skip a beat every time. Because of her nonstop work schedule, they could not enjoy an actual evening out. Instead, he showed up in the parking lot of Benedicts' every afternoon at three. He had something new and fun to do every day. Movies, picnics on the floor of a limo, rowing, video arcades.

He had never approached her at the restaurant during working hours before. He'd made plans for that afternoon, but Robin had begged off, exhausted from the double shift she'd worked at Benedicts'. She wondered if canceling their date is what prompted this impromptu meeting.

"Tell me something," he said, reaching under the table and pulling her feet into his lap. Before she could protest, he had slipped off her shoes and his fingers and thumbs suddenly did the most delicious things to her arches.

"Hmmm?" Unable to stop herself, she melted into the chair and leaned her head back, closing her eyes.

"I've been paying attention to that little tip jar you have on the bar, not to mention the credit card tips and the cash the customers hand you personally."

She opened an eye and looked at him from under her lashes. "So?"

"So, between Benedicts' and here, six days a week for both of them, you make a tidy sum."

Robin could barely concentrate on his words. His hands felt so powerful and so tender all at once. She didn't have the energy to do anything more than enjoy the foot rub. Last night she'd gotten exactly four point two hours of sleep. As she sat there, she had a minimum of eight hours in front of her. "What about it?"

"Are you on drugs?"

She opened one eye. "Don't irritate me when you're doing that with your hands." His fingers inched up her calves now, kneading and soothing. Robin had no idea how much her calf muscles ached until he rubbed the ache right out of them.

"I was just wondering why someone who makes what you make in tips in a single day, combined with what Maxine would have started making at the barest minimum, why you would live in the apartment you live in, and drive around in that hunk of junk you drive that isn't going to start one night out here at one o'clock in the morning." His voice became steely, but his hands stayed soothing, gentle with just the right amount of pressure.

She spoke without thinking about it. "Tuition."

His hands paused for the first time since he started talking. "What tuition?"

She opened her eyes, slowly sat up and drew her feet from his lap. "Sarah's." Under the table, her feet sought out her shoes and wiggled back into them.

He stared at her. "The numbers don't add up, Robin. Maxine easily makes—"

"Stay out of it, Tony. It's truly none of your business."

His eyes flashed while his jaw tightened. "I'm making it my business."

She stood and pulled her peppermints out of her pocket. "Not until I do." He opened his mouth to speak, but she held a hand up to halt him. "No. Not everyone can wake up with the luxury of knowing they have enough money in the bank to never go hungry, to never be cold, to never have to worry about transportation for the rest of their lives." She stood and downed the remaining coffee in one swallow and popped a mint into her mouth.

"You think I don't know that?" He sat back a bit and crossed his arms across his thick chest.

"I think you have it so good that it's easy to wake up in your penthouse apartment and forget that there are mortals down below you who have to struggle while you send your blessings up to a god who lets children starve." She slapped both palms on the table and leaned forward. "I vowed that I would get my sisters through school. Me. Not with anyone's help, not even from them. They would have the chance at a life that our mother wasn't going to allow. I put Maxi through, and I'm putting Sarah through, and forget anyone who says I shouldn't or I can't or I look piqued when I do."

He stood as well and leaned forward until they stood nearly nose-to-nose. "Don't try to place me in a category, Robin. I won't fit."

She snorted and straightened. "Careful, Antonio Viscolli. You'll choke on your silver spoon."

The heat in his eyes made her feel a little bit frightened for a split second, then he muttered something in Italian under his breath and came over the table to her side and grabbed her arm. "Come with me."

She struggled to free herself, but it was no use. "What are you doing?" she sputtered, clawing at his hand. "Let me go!"

"I'd rather not make a scene," he explained through gritted teeth while he eyed the suddenly still kitchen. He slammed open the back door and pulled her outside. A waiter crouched against a crate, a book in one hand and a cup of coffee in the other. His expression remained pleasant when he looked up at them. "Take over the bar for this shift, will you, Rob?"

The man stood up straight. "Sure. Sure, Mr. V."

Robin sputtered. "No way. Get your hands off me." Tony's stride never broke and he continued to haul her across the parking lot. "I'm not going anywhere with you. Do you hear me?" Nothing. "I'll scream for help."

He stopped so suddenly that she ran into his back. He turned her until she faced him, and he gripped both of her arms. "Do it."

She heard the very real threat in his voice. Not wanting to risk it, she clamped her lips together and stiffly shook her head. "Good. Now, get in the car."

She tried to stare him down, but eventually lost the battle, and with half a growl, she threw herself into the seat. Seconds later, Tony sat beside her, starting the powerful engine of the little sports car, and tearing out of the parking lot.

"Where are we going?"

"I have something to show you."

"I hope you realize that you just hauled your best bartender out of your bar on the busiest night of the week." She crossed her arms over her chest and glared out the window.

"Hank's isn't going to collapse because Robin Bartlett isn't manning the bar for one Saturday night. As a matter of fact, it would still be there without a bar." He took a corner fast enough to make her shoulder lean on the door.

"I'm losing tips."

"I'll give you a raise."

"I don't want a raise."

"But you deserve a raise. You're my best bartender."

In a rage now, she slapped the dashboard. "You can't just drag someone around like that and force them to do your bidding. I don't care who you are or how much money you…"

"Robin," he said very quietly, but with enough ice to halt her screaming sentence, "I'm warning you, now, to just clam it."

She decided to save it until they got to wherever he was taking them. The longer she remained quiet, the more calmly he drove. In the late afternoon light, Robin recognized landmarks and realized they had traveled into a pretty rough section of town. She remembered, all too vividly, living as a child and a young teenager in many of the apartment buildings they passed. Deep into one of the worst neighborhoods she knew of, he casually pulled into the parking lot of a large church. Robin knew the church. It took up two full blocks with all of its buildings and schools. As a little girl, she had always used it as a major landmark.

"Why are we here?" she asked, trying not to let her apprehension creep into her voice.

Tony didn't speak for several moments. Finally, he said, "I apologize, sincerely, for losing my temper." He turned off the car and got out, moving slower than usual as he came around to her side to open her door. As soon as she was out of the car, he took her hand in his. "My feelings for you tend to override a lot of things. Please accept my apology."

His feelings for her? Reeling over the last several minutes, Robin could do nothing but nod and stammer, "Okay."

His smile did not quite reach his eyes. "Let's walk."

Robin looked all around her. "Uh, Tony, this isn't really the best neighborhood -"

Tony clenched his jaw. "Robin, *cara mia*, not everything in life is a debate. Could you, just once today, stop arguing with me? If it wouldn't be too much trouble?"

Robin closed her mouth. Whatever retort she had

prepared vanished in a heartbeat. She sensed that he intended to share something important with her. She suddenly wanted to know what that important thing might be.

He led them away from the church. "Let me tell you a story."

"Really, that isn't—"

"Once upon a time, there was a young sixteen-year-old girl who fell in love with a fisherman in Florence, Italy. He was much older than her, and well below her station, but she didn't care. Thumbing her nose at her parents, she married him, anyway. They told her to never come back and disowned her." Tony steered her around the legs of a snoring man who sat against a building, empty bottle gripped in his dirty hands, and continued his story.

"Well, for about a year, life was bliss. Until the day a storm hit right off the coast and took the fisherman with it. She was young, devastated, alone, and pregnant. Not to mention poor. She tried to go to her parents for help, but they were true to their word and wouldn't even open the door to her. Now, her husband didn't have any family in Italy, but he spoke often of his Aunt Rosa in America. See, that was his dream. To eventually raise enough money to take his family away from the poverty that had trapped him in Italy and bring them to America."

Robin scooted closer to Tony as they passed a hooker with mean eyes. He squeezed her hand and kept talking. "She wrote Rosa, sold everything she could to raise enough money to get here, and came on her way. She had expected the grand American life, and was crushed when she learned that Rosa was actually even more poor than she was, and lived in an apartment that didn't even have a working heater half the time. She was miserable, very pregnant, and sleeping on a sofa in a cold two-room apartment. And Rosa was old. She was actually her husband's great aunt.

"Neither women spoke English, and she had a hard time finding a job. Now, in this neighborhood, there were several things a woman could do to earn money, few of which are legal, and she went that route, falling victim to a few vices along the way. Her son stayed with Rosa while she went about her life, popping in and out every so often. Then she'd leave and do whatever it was that she did to support her heroin addiction."

Robin knew, without a doubt, that the little boy in the story was Antonio Viscolli. Shamed at the way she'd spoken to him, at what she said, she suddenly didn't want to hear the rest of the story. "Tony…"

The look in his eyes and his single raised finger stilled her. "Wait. I'm almost to the punch line. Anyway, Rosa died when the boy was ten. He was in school, but only in the second grade, because he was having to learn English as he went. His mother showed up to claim the apartment, and having a young son did nothing to hamper her lifestyle. Life was hell for him, but he managed to make it on his own. Of course, rent had to be paid and food had to be bought, so, following the path of his mother, he hit the streets. He wasn't very big and could get in and out of an apartment quickly. He made some pretty good contacts and could fence a television for a good price. He even hit the business section a few times, got caught by the police twice picking pockets, and was pretty much headed toward becoming a hoodlum."

She couldn't imagine Tony doing any of that. Looking at him, dressed to the nines in his suit, his shirt perfectly starched and gleaming white, his tie straight, the diamond on his pinkie catching the glow of the afternoon sun—he looked every single bit of the rich businessman. No way could she picture him worming his way out of a window carrying a pilfered radio.

They stopped now, next to a dilapidated old building with boarded up windows. Tony turned to face her. The smooth cultured look vanished in a breath. His eyes had hardened. His mouth pulled into a thin line. Even his voice had changed. It sounded harsher, carried an accent that was a mix of Italian, South Boston, and insolence. "He found his mother dead when he was seventeen. She'd overdosed on her favorite drug. The needle was still sticking out of her arm." He stepped away from her and looked over her shoulder down the street. "The landlord had already taped the eviction notice on the door, so without a backward look, he left.

"He was just out of juvie, so none of his so-called friends trusted him. Too many came out narks at first, so he had no place to stay." He came toward her again and put an arm over her shoulder, turning her so that she was facing the building. He pointed toward the doorway. "That was a good place to sleep. It has a deep recess and a stoop. It blocked the wind, which was good, because January is bitter cold."

Robin's stomach muscles shivered, as if she personally felt that cold. Her voice quivered and her throat ached with unshed tears. "That's enough."

"No. It isn't." He turned her until they were looking down the street. "There's an Italian restaurant down that way. They make good calzones. The wife used to make all the pasta by hand. The guy, he'd throw enough food away at night so that anyone hungry enough, right after he went inside, could hit the Dumpster and fight off the cats and rats and get himself something to eat."

"Stop!" She put a hand over her mouth and stared at him.

"I laid there in that doorway one night. It couldn't have been more than twenty degrees. I was cold, starving, exhausted, and I swore that I would die before I suffered through one more night. I swore that would be the very last night. And, miracle of miracles, it was." He turned them back the way they came and they headed back toward the tall steeples of the church. "The next night, I went into the church. I decided I'd case the place, see what I could get for what I could get. There was some service going on in there. I walked in right at the end of the singing and right before the preaching.

"Robin, I cannot put into human words what happened to me when I heard that pastor's message of salvation. It was like a dam burst and a floodgate of love poured into and out of my heart. The message that God loved me, that I wasn't alone, that no matter how cold I got or how hungry I got, He would provide a way for me. I'd been alone my entire life and suddenly, someone loved me. Me. A bad kid with a chip on his shoulder the size of the bay. A low life thief."

One of his eyebrows raised to emphasize his next words. "A liar." He paused as if to let that sink in; as if lying were worse than stealing or thuggery.

"I learned the most important thing of all, that no matter what I did up until that moment, I was forgiven. The almighty, all-powerful, all-knowing God who created the universe and time knew everything I had ever done, every thought I ever had, and He still loved me and forgave me. As if I had never done any of it, as if I had never thought any of it. He forgave ME and he loved ME."

He put his hands on her shoulders. "It's hard for those of us who never had any good parenting models to grasp, but we are His children and He loves each one of us so much that He sent His own Son to die for us. Robin, He loves you as much as He loves me."

CHAPTER NINE

Robin **felt a tingling in** the back of her chest, near her stomach. She took a deep breath hoping the cool evening air would still whatever strange sensation flooded her body. It didn't. Hearing that God, a being whom she didn't even know whether she believed existed, loved her made her want to cry and beg, but she didn't know why she should cry or for what she should beg. Instead, she ignored the intensity of the feeling and refocused on Tony's story. "What happened?"

Tony saw her fight the battle inside herself, the battle between flesh and spirit, and witnessed her flesh win. He knew Robin didn't win, though. Fighting back against the knocking of the Holy Spirit did nothing but place her on the losing side. He fervently prayed while he gently put a hand on her elbow and continued walking.

Robin could sense Tony's disappointment, but it confused her. She thought maybe he regretted telling her the story. She had never told anyone, ever, how she had lived, what she had endured. As far as it concerned her, nothing that happened to her before today had anything to do with anyone else. She wanted to rub his arm and tell him that she could forget everything he said and they could go back to the lighthearted fun they'd had all week.

They reached the church again but instead of taking her back to the car, he steered them onto a tree-lined residential street. The street didn't fit in the neighborhood. The freshly painted houses sported cute little lawns and picket fences. Kids' toys and bicycles sat propped against trees and chalk drawings decorated the sidewalks.

Rather than tell her what happened next, Tony decided to let her experience a small taste of it. He gestured. "The church owns this street. The staff lives here. Surprisingly, the crime in this neighborhood has never made its way down this row. I think the church does so much that no one wants to hurt the people who help." He winked at her, "Or there's an angel guarding the entrance. It could go either way."

Dusk settled around them and porch lights carved through the twilight. They walked about halfway down the street and Tony stopped Robin and unlatched a picket gate. How many times over the years had he reached down and lifted that latch? Thousands? When he felt overwhelmed, he came home to this place. When he felt frustrated, he lifted that little latch and walked down the little stone path. When the darts and arrows of the world overcame him, he would find solace and comfort beyond the picket fence. He suddenly realized that never, in all of his years, had he brought a female guest with him. Especially a female for whom he had such strong feelings. He realized that they would see it right away, and he grinned at the thought.

He led the way down the little path to the front door. Instead of opening it with the key in his pocket, he rang the doorbell and stepped back. The sounds from inside made him smile. Every single thing in his life might change, but everything here would always remain the same.

As he rang the bell, Robin could hear laughter, loud voices, running feet. A woman opened the door. Tendrils of hair escaped her ponytail and tickled the large freckles scattered across her cheeks, forehead, and nose. She had her long dress covered by an apron and fuzzy pink bunny house slippers on her feet. She looked maybe ten years older than Tony.

"*Buona sera*," Tony said.

"What in the world are you doing ringing the doorbell?" She asked, her eyes skimming over Tony then resting on Robin. "Ah. I see." She put her hands on her hips and smiled at Tony while she tried to act stern. "I don't see you or hear from you all week and you show up when I have on bunny slippers and no makeup!"

Tony smiled. "You're beautiful, *amica*."

She blushed and laughed before opening the door wider. "Please come in."

He stepped aside and put a hand on the small of Robin's back, steering her in front of him. "This is Robin Bartlett. Robin, allow me to introduce Caroline O'Farrell."

Caroline held her hand out in a very welcoming manner. Robin couldn't help feeling that she genuinely liked meeting her. "Pleasure to meet you, Robin." She looked wryly over Robin's head toward Tony. "Tony's never brought a girl home before."

Robin didn't know what to say and tried to resist

Tony's pressure on her back to step forward. She lost that momentary battle and finally took her offered hand and allowed her to pull her into the house. "It's nice to meet you, Caroline. Sorry to pop in without calling first."

"Don't be silly. Don't need to announce Tony. He's one of us." They went from the small entryway into a good-sized living room. Books and puzzles spilled out of a bookshelf onto the carpeted floor. Framed pictures of children in various ages and ethnicities and general kiddish cuteness covered the walls. A white teenage boy and a younger black teenage girl sprawled on a sofa in front of a television. A little boy with tawny hair and round glasses carried plates to the table that filled the other half of the room. A little girl of Oriental descent came darting from the open kitchen door screaming, "Uncle Tony! Uncle Tony!"

He grinned as he bent to pick her up, swinging her around and kissing both cheeks. "Little Angel Dove. How are you?"

"I have a loose tooth," she said, then promptly bared her teeth and pushed her front tooth forward with her tongue. "I'll get a dollar when it comes out!"

Tony showed exactly the right amount of interest. "A whole dollar?"

"Yep!"

"What will you do with a whole dollar?"

"Well," she said, rolling her eyes to look at Caroline, "mom says that a whole dime of it has to go to church. That will leave enough for at least a pack of gum, she said."

"At least." He kissed her temple before setting her down. "Haven't I taught you the art of negotiation?"

Caroline laughed. "We started at fifty cents."

Smiling, Tony patted Angel's head. "That's my girl."

A tall thin man with salt-and-pepper hair and black framed glasses came out of the kitchen and walked straight toward them with a smile on his face. His white apron sported giant red lips and the words "KISS THE COOK". In one hand he held grilling tongs and the other a bottle of barbecue sauce. He set them both on the table as he passed by it and had his arms out before he even reached them.

"Tony, my brother!" he said with great enthusiasm.

"Peter, *mio fratello*, it's great to see you," Tony said. He stepped forward. With interest, Robin watched the two men embrace and pound each other on the back as they broke contact. The smile on Tony's face removed the last of the traces of harshness the neighborhood had brought earlier. "I'd like you to meet someone," Tony said, turning to bring Robin into their fold. "Robin Bartlett, this is my good friend and brother, Peter O'Farrell. Peter, this is Robin."

Behind the black rimmed glasses, Peter's brow lifted with a keen interest but he didn't say anything except, "It's a pleasure to meet you, my dear. You two will be staying for dinner, then." He didn't ask, merely stated, and despite the fact that she had just recently inhaled a bread bowl filled with chili and half a slice of pecan pie, Robin found herself following the adults into the kitchen and out the back door to a little patio looking out over a backyard strewn with balls and bikes. On the small concrete slab, a large charcoal grill smoked away.

A fence didn't enclose the back yard like it did the front yard. Similar patios stretched out on either side and Robin could see church buildings in front of her in the fading light. Between the church and the rows of houses, she could make out a large children's playground and a volleyball net. Well-tended and somewhat worn bricked pathways led from the church buildings to the playground.

Peter had collected his supplies on their way out of the house. He lifted the lid on the grill and used a set of tongs to poke at some chicken thighs that lay spread out on the hot rack. As he fussed with the meat, he spoke to Tony. "Haven't heard from you all week. Figured you'd headed south a bit early."

Tony offered Robin a plastic chair. As she and Caroline sat next to each other, he made his way to Peter's side. "I've been otherwise occupied," he said smiling.

Peter glanced around Tony to Robin. "With work?"

"Not exactly." Tony put a hand on Robin's shoulder. She didn't realize how tense she felt until his touch drew it out of her. She slowly relaxed. "How was the conference?"

Caroline answered. "Antonio, it was wonderful! The more we can get the word out there, the better it will be for all of the children."

Tony caught Robin's eye and explained, "Peter and Caroline, on top of all of their other duties at the church, run a nonprofit corporation that helps people financially with adoption."

"What do you do at the church?" Robin asked.

"I teach the youth," Peter said.

Caroline snorted. "Don't let him be modest with you. He runs the youth department. He has about 900 children."

Robin's eyes grew wide. "Wow. What do you do?"

"As our department has grown, I have less time for a lot of hands-on and spend most of my time in administration, managing the pastors and teachers of the kids," he said, poking at a thigh. "Back when I first met Tony, we had about a third of the numbers we have now, and I actually taught down in the trenches."

Tony interjected. "Peter and I met the night I was saved; the night I was just telling you about. He took me to the gymnasium, let me grab a shower and gave me a change of clothes."

Peter laughed and interrupted. "That's because you smelled so bad."

Tony laughed and continued, "And then brought me here. Caroline fed me…"

This time Caroline interrupted. "Corned beef and cabbage. Food fit for a man." She looked at Robin with a wink. "About the only thing I can cook and not burn."

"…then they gave me a bedroom."

Robin looked up at Tony, who still had a hand on her shoulder. "Just like that?"

Caroline answered again. "When we're Spirit led, it's often just like that."

"Spirit led?"

Caroline's questioning eyes shot toward Tony, who ignored her. "Peter got me a job as a janitor at the church. I lived here and worked for a year."

This time Peter interrupted. "I appointed him as a custodial engineer. When he wasn't working, he was in the church library reading. I think he only came here to sleep."

Tony smiled. "And eat."

"As only a teenaged boy can," Caroline said with a laugh.

"What did you read?" Robin could not help feeling intrigued by Tony's past, by his path.

"Anything and everything. I read the Bible three times that year. I read every word I could get my hands on to explain what I'd read. I watched every documentary they had on the shelves and went to every service I could go to."

"Hungry boy," Caroline said.

Peter finally finished prodding and started turning the meat over. "He saved every dime he made, too. Wore clothes out of the clothes closet so that he wouldn't have to buy any, even."

Tony remembered. Ill-fitting pants and baggy shirts on his skinny frame. "My eighteenth birthday was fast approaching. I had to save."

"How did you…" Robin stopped short of asking, but Tony knew what she wanted to ask. How did he go from skinny waif to healthy and muscular, wealthy and successful, polished and proper?

"He took everything he made," Peter started, but his wife interrupted him.

"Prayed over it," she said.

Peter continued, "then put it all into a computer company on the stock market."

"You made your money in the stock market?"

Tony moved until he stood in front of her so that she wouldn't have to crane her neck to see him. "No. I made quite a bit of money off of my investment and then used that to buy a bookstore. The store was floundering, badly, and I got it for a fraction of its worth. Very quickly, I turned it around and used the profits from there to buy a bankrupt auto parts store. Very soon, I could buy a franchise of a fast food restaurant and…"

Caroline stood. "Everything that man touched turned to gold. Before a decade passed, he probably couldn't even tell you all of the different companies and corporations and franchises he owned."

Tony cut his eyes to her. "Sure I could." He looked back at Robin. "I stayed faithful to God, and He stayed faithful to me. I tithed with passion, studied the Bible with passion, prayed over every business venture I made, and God continued to bless me."

Robin opened her mouth to speak, but Tony didn't let her ask the "why" question he could tell was on her lips. "He continued to bless me because there's work to be done. Unfortunately, in order to work, you need to have money. He must have trusted me not to make an idol of money, and to pour forth as much as I could back into work for His kingdom."

He could tell she didn't understand. "My objective has never been to be rich and powerful. It has merely been to never be cold and hungry again. God took my drive and my faithfulness and used both to help others through me. To fiscally help this church and a dozen others like it, to donate to charities, to get kids off of the streets and into proper homes." Forgetting his friends, he knelt next to her chair. "If only you and I had ever had access to what my foundation does today, how different would our lives have been, eh?"

Robin felt that swirling, tingling feeling in her stomach again. She didn't know if Tony sitting so close to her or this deity to whom they all referred to and obviously revered caused the feeling. "If you'd had access, however, you wouldn't have your drive and we wouldn't be here today, would we?"

Caroline slapped her knee as she stood up. "Ha! That is a good point, there." She went to her husband and slipped an arm around his waist. "Need a platter for the bird, love?"

"That would be wonderful. Thank you."

Before long, Robin found herself sitting at a table with the entire family. She learned that Caroline and Peter adopted all but the oldest boy. After the entire table held hands and Peter said a long prayer over their food, they ate the chicken with potato salad and baked beans that came from a grocery store deli. Despite the size of the meal she'd had at Hank's, Robin found herself enjoying this one immensely. She had no experience with interacting in this setting of family dynamics, but she enjoyed observing them.

The biggest mystery she kept coming back to, though, was that Tony fit in with them. Never in a million years would she have guessed that he came from such humble roots. Never would she have thought that he spent Sunday afternoons after church in this living room with this family. She had always imagined him wining and dining in penthouse apartments or yachts on the Bay or mansions on the hill. However, here, in this little home with the picket fence out front, here is where he fit—perfectly fit—his hand-tailored shirt and twenty-four karat cuff links notwithstanding.

After the meal and after Caroline dispatched children to the kitchen to tackle the dishes, the adults moved to the living room with cake and coffee and talked. Robin enjoyed while Caroline and Peter bombarded her with stories of young Tony. She watched him interact with them, watched him completely relax as he leaned against the cushions and smiled at some story about him trying to learn Greek so that he could read the Bible in Greek.

"Turns out, I'm more inclined toward Latin," he punned.

She sat next to him and he turned his head slightly, looking away from Peter and toward her. As their eyes met, his smile slowly and gradually left his face. He looked very solemn, very serious. Robin felt pulled into his stare until even Peter's voice came from far away. Tony gently ran a finger down her cheek then took her hand in his. Robin felt a flutter in her heart. As soon as Tony broke eye contact with her and laughed at something Caroline said, the room came back into focus. She tried to pick up in her mind where the conversation left off, tried to pull her fingers out from his grasp, but he just entwined their fingers and squeezed.

It felt right to sit with him like this so she settled back into the couch and enjoyed the stories, and the company, and the... love... that just flowed all around her.

CHAPTER TEN

Robin found herself very restless on Sunday. She'd hoped she would spend the day with Tony, but after leaving the O'Farrell's with him Saturday night and getting dropped off at her apartment door with nothing more than a smile and an invitation to attend church the next day—which she declined—she didn't hear from him.

She paced her apartment, cleaned out her closet, worried about doing laundry and missing his call, paced some more, and as the sun faded in the sky she found herself sitting on her couch staring mindlessly at some nature documentary and feeling a little blue. With Maxine on a date and Sarah at her parents' house, she found herself feeling lonely, too. With her schedule, living with her two sisters, and constantly having to interact with people, she had always enjoyed solitude.

Had she done or said something to offend Tony? Did he not like the way she reacted to his story? Did he regret introducing her to his friends?

Turning the television off in disgust, she surged to her feet. She would not be reduced to this emotional state of neediness by a man. She had survived twenty-six years without Antonio Viscolli, and she'd go on surviving without him.

Working herself into a good angry fit, she decided she would go ahead and do laundry, whether that meant that she'd miss his phone call or not. Not that she expected him to call this late, anyway. While she sorted her laundry and shoved it all into a bag, she muttered to herself all of the reasons why she'd spent so many years avoiding a relationship with anyone.

As she walked down to the laundry room and, with way more force than the chore required, shoved her clothes into the available washers, she built herself back up, reminding her inner self that she had tuition to pay, rent coming due, a car about to die on her. A man, or a relationship with a man, or a non-relationship with a man, did not fit into her schedule in any way at the moment.

With three machines loudly chugging away at her clothes, she left the laundry room with much less furor than she had entered it. She slowly walked up the flights of stairs to her apartment and let herself back in. As she contemplated maybe fixing something to eat, she noticed the red light blinking on the answering machine, signaling an incoming message.

Her heart skipped a beat before it started pounding. She rushed to push the button and felt an immediate deflation of emotion as she heard Hank's gravelly voice.

"Robin? Hank. I need to talk with you before your Benedicts' shift tomorrow. Ten is a good time. If you have to work breakfast first, try to just make it as soon as you can. No need to call me back unless it's to tell me a better time. Thanks. Have a good night."

Never, in all of the years that she'd worked for him, had Hank ever called her in to meet with her. Frowning at the answering machine, Robin replayed the message, trying to glean some hint as to what he could possibly want to talk about with her. He'd pulled her into his office too many times to count for various reasons over the years—checking on her, she knew. Making sure she was emotionally handling everything in her life to his satisfaction. She allowed it because she loved him. Despite that, never had he called her at home, nor asked her to come in for a scheduled meeting while off shift.

After a night spent tossing and turning and tossing some more, worrying about Hank's call and fretting over the lack of a call from Tony, she finally quit trying to sleep and got up early. She braided her long hair, dressed in the first uniform of the week, her Benedicts' lunch uniform, and headed to Hank's.

Hank's did not open until four on Mondays. Instead of a lunch shift, the kitchen staff received orders, stocked shelves, freezers, and refrigerators, and planned specials for the week. As Robin came in through the kitchen door, she had to twist aside to avoid colliding with a harried produce salesman who stamped quickly away from Casey's rage over, she assumed, the asparagus he clutched in both hands and held above his head.

Instead of exchanging their standard greeting, she avoided becoming Casey's target in the absence of the salesman and headed straight to Hank's office. She rapped her knuckles on the closed door in quick succession, waited for the barked command to enter, and opened the door. As she opened the door, she had to step aside as two men in paint-splattered coveralls left the room. When Robin entered, she stopped short to find Tony seated behind the desk and Hank in one of the chairs before it. The bare walls no longer sported photos of Hank in the Navy, plaques, awards, or posters. Instead, fresh white paint glared back and made the room seem smaller. The standard piles and stacks of papers and books no longer cluttered the top of the desk. The bookshelf had all personal knickknacks and Tom Clancy novels removed and in their place sat books whose spines bragged of financial or management success.

She took all of this in as she came farther into the room, but it confused her. Her understanding was that Hank would stay for a few years. "What's up?" she said. She looked at Hank first, then Tony, then back to Hank.

Hank spoke. "Jessica, my youngest daughter, fell down the stairs Saturday night and broke her femur."

Robin gasped and took the chair next to him. "Oh no."

"Marjorie's already there. She needed to go down and take care of the baby."

"Of course."

"I called Tony on Sunday and we've been here since five this morning working everything out."

Robin shifted her attention from Hank to Tony. "What everything?"

Tony didn't look like he'd been at the office since five. His shirt looked crisp, freshly starched, and his blue tie speckled with tiny gold ichthuses looked sharp against the whiteness of the shirt. "Hank is declining the five-year management position. He's decided to go ahead and leave."

Robin saw little bright lights in front of her eyes as a

little swirl of panic start spinning in her chest. "I—ah…"

Hank reached over and engulfed her hand in his. "Marjorie didn't like that clause, and she and I have been trying to come to a compromise about it. When the contracts changing ownership of the restaurant were signed, we kept it open. Jessica's going to be down and out for a long time. With her husband's ship deployed, there's nothing else we can do but go be there for her and help her."

Little beads of moisture formed on her upper lip. "But _"

Tony leaned back in his chair. His fingers fidgeted with the gold pen that lay on the clean white blotter in front of him. "Hank and I have spent the last few weeks immersed in personnel and personalities and positions. He and I are both in agreement."

"Agreement?" Did she miss a chunk of the conversation?

"Effective today, the bar is closed." As if on cue, Robin heard the sound of a saw fire up from somewhere in the restaurant. "We're tearing it out and opening up more seating in its place."

A little tinge of irritation helped slow down the spiral of panic. "Great." She'd known it was coming, though. The news didn't surprise her. Only, she still hadn't figured out what she'd do instead. "I guess I have the evening free, then."

Tony smiled. "As nice as that prospect is, I'm afraid that you're going to be a little busier than normal."

"Oh? Why is that?"

"I need to go out to California. I have a venture there that's still on shaky ground, and there's a hotel in

Manhattan that I'm in the preliminary negotiations with that's going to start taking up a lot of my personal time." He spun the gold pen between his fingers like a tiny baton while he studied her face.

With shaking hands, Robin pulled her tin of mints out of her pocket and popped one in her mouth. "Look—you don't need to explain."

He tilted his head and gave her a confused look. "No. Let me finish." He hooked a foot over his knee. "Here's the problem. Hank's leaving about a month earlier than anticipated. We tried to look at resumes for a manager but neither of us were pleased with what we've seen out there. None of them have what I'm looking for."

She felt the frown crease her brow. "What's that?"

His eyes burned with a serious intensity while he looked at her. "Your experience. Your love of this place. Your drive."

She blinked. "Excuse me?"

"I talked it over with Hank. He's in complete agreement."

Hank squeezed her hand and released her. "Absolutely."

"Complete agreement about what?"

Tony quit spinning the pen and smiled a very charming smile. "About you."

A kind of fearful excitement tried to course through her veins, but she stamped it down. "What are you getting at?"

"I want you to run Hank's for me. I want to hire you on as the manager so that I don't have to worry about losing what it is that makes it Hank's."

She snorted. "Yeah, right."

"I'm absolutely serious."

She looked in his eyes and saw that he was. "Look, Tony. I'm just a barmaid, a waitress, and a high school dropout. You don't want me running this place for you."

"What does any of that have to do with anything? A person with your experience?" He felt the anger and only partially tried to keep it in check. "I didn't ask you about your educational background."

"Well, it's a good thing you didn't. I've never even gotten my GED."

"So?"

Now she laughed. "So, hire some guy who has a bunch of education and is trained for the position. A Viscolli company doesn't need some two-bit bartender running anything for it."

Tony's temperature rose a few degrees. He felt as if, in insulting her, she had personally insulted him. No one talked about Robin that way. "You think that I give 'two bits' about diplomas and accolades? If I wanted that, I could have had my pick all week. I want you."

Robin looked from one man to the other and felt heat flood her cheeks, trying to find the right words. "Look, Tony. If you're doing this just because we—"

He cut her off. "Robin, one of the reasons I'm what I am is because I don't mix my business and personal life. It will cut you off at the knees every time."

"You'll be laughed out of the Chamber of Commerce if you hire me."

"You think?" Taking a different approach, he slowly stood. "Do you think I'm qualified to run my company?"

Obviously not liking his advantage, she stood as well. "Obviously."

"I used to Dumpster dive to eat my one meal a day," he chided. Instead of continuing on, he took a deep breath and closed his eyes, praying to find the right words. "My point, *cara mia*, is that if the Chamber of Commerce were going to find something to laugh at me about, it wouldn't be because I picked the best, most qualified person in this entire city to run my newly acquired restaurant."

His words, the naked sincerity that weighed them down, penetrated Robin's very blood and beat through her veins in a rush. Robin had needed the reminder. Wow! She thought she hadn't forgotten, really, what he had disclosed about his past on Saturday. Somehow, though, she could barely reconcile those facts with this Tony; smooth, cultured, in charge. He commanded the room even over Hank.

When Tony talked about having to go to California and New York, she thought he'd been in the midst of firing her and ending their relationship. Now she had an opportunity to work even closer with him. That prospect alone promised some really unexplainable appeal for her.

Could she let herself harbor some tiny hope that even she could rise above her own personal birthright? Could someone one day meet her and not believe how she had lived her whole life? Would she one day find herself transformed as completely as a caterpillar to a butterfly? As completely changed as Tony had changed? Could she become a brand-new creature?

She sat, looked between the two men again. "What now?"

Tony admired his own personal restraint that kept him

from throwing back his head and laughing with glee. "Now, you look over my offer, the contract, haggle over the salary, get at least fifteen percent more, then you go to dinner with me tonight to celebrate your new promotion at work."

Hank's laugh reminded her of his presence. "I will take that as my leave to go. I have a lot of packing to do. Tony," he held his hand out and Tony leaned over the desk to shake it. "It has been an absolute joy to work with you."

"And you, sir. May God bless you and keep you."

He looked at Robin as he sat back down. "You still look a little dazed. I'm going to give you a draft of the contract and let you read over it. I need you to put in your notice at Benedicts'. This is more than a full-time job."

"I can't afford -"

Tony felt the smile on his face, excited for her, anticipating her surprise over the salary offered. He had left the contract writing up to Barry, so even though he'd have personally padded it just because he loved her, Barry didn't and nothing was nonstandard. Even so, he had a feeling that the number hovering just under six figures would more than satisfy her current living situation, tuition notwithstanding.

"Just take this and read it. If you have any questions, I'll be happy to answer them." He held out the eight-page contract and waited for her to reach out and take it.

She stood as she did and said, "Okay. Thank you." She turned to leave, as if dismissed or dismissing him. He wanted her to stay with him and chat some more. He wanted to spend a portion of this insane morning with the soothing calm of her presence.

"How was your day off?" he asked.

Robin spun around. Her eyes flashed anger, w. confused him a little bit, but her voice remained ca. "Fine."

"What did you do with your time?"

"Nothing," she said, rolling up the bound pages in her hand. "Absolutely nothing."

Tony raised an eyebrow, thinking that he'd discovered the root of the anger. "Is there something specifically wrong that you'd like to talk about?"

Robin advanced on him, waving the rolled-up contract in front of her like a rapier. "You take me out every single day for a week. I work two jobs and in the brief hours each day I normally have to decompress and refocus my energies, I ended up with you. Suddenly, on the one day off I have for the entire week, I don't hear a word."

Ah. Clarity. "I asked if you wanted to come to church with me."

"Because I declined the offer to go to church with you, you blow me off for the entire day?"

"Of course not. I don't just put on a tie and spend an hour in a building, Robin. My entire Sunday is spent in holy communion with God. There are two services on Sundays, and as the treasurer of the church board, I had a presentation to give to the church body regarding some land acquisitions, so I stayed for both services. I also teach a Sunday School class. By the time I leave the church building, it's late afternoon and I typically end up in the home of one of the staff members, enjoy a light lunch and some low-key fellowship, then head back into the church building for evening worship."

As he spoke he watched her face fuse with color. Tony stood and moved quickly around the desk so that he could

_n her, take her hand in his and look into
_poke. "I wanted to spend the day with you.
_out you all day long. I wished you'd been there
_e music, to listen to the amazing sermon that I
_wice, to have lunch with me and my friends."

Robin felt her hand momentarily tremble in his. The
back of her throat burned and she had no idea why. She
cleared her throat and pulled her hand away. "Okay. I'm
sorry that I was so upset."

Before she could turn back around, he grabbed her
hand again. "You're still a little upset. I'm sorry that you
didn't understand what my Sunday is like. I should have
been more clear. While I enjoy thinking about you wanting
to hear from me, I don't enjoy having unintentionally let
you down or hurt you in any way."

Robin looked into his eyes and saw the sincerity
and—something else. Something warm, wonderful,
inviting. She saw safety, security, peace. Her heart started
pounding. Blood roared in her ears. She wondered how he
couldn't hear it, it sounded so loud.

He stood close enough that she could feel the heat of
his body. Even so, she wanted to be closer to him still. She
stepped forward until the tips of their shoes touched. Not
knowing which one of them made the move to close the
last of the gap, she found herself wrapped in his arms, his
mouth on hers.

The initial punch in his gut from finally holding her and
touching her spread until his whole body fairly tingled with
want to get closer to her. Her cool lips almost immediately
warmed under his, softened for him. He forcefully pushed
back his desire and instead just reveled in the amazing feel
of her lips, of her hands on his back, of her scent that

surrounded him.

She was tired, worn out, still disturbed by unfamiliar emotions which had assaulted her for a steac week. That was the reason her head started spinning, why her limbs trembled. His mouth felt hot, demanding. Wonderful.

His teeth nipped and she gasped. Taking advantage of her open mouth, his tongue swept inside. A feeling she didn't recognize streaked straight to her stomach and her knees buckled. His arm caught her weight, pulled her closer until his body pressed against hers.

He pulled away when she whimpered. The sound was so small, so desperate, that he sensed enough was enough. While he was willing to release her mouth, he wasn't quite ready to release her altogether. He pressed his lips to her forehead, then pulled her face to his chest.

His heart pounded under her ear. She should have felt embarrassed, now that the room had stopped tilting. Instead, she was in awe over the fact that simply kissing her had caused such a reaction in him. His strong arms held her, secure, and for just a moment, she let herself seep into him, let herself lean into his strength.

Then reality came flooding back.

He sensed it the instant before her body tensed. With great reluctance, he relaxed his arms and stepped back.

"I'm sorry," she said, stepping backward until there were at least two feet between them.

Tony laughed. "I'm not. I've been wanting to do that since we met."

Her lips felt a little numb and a lot tingly. She resisted the urge to touch them. "I need to go to work now."

.d picked up the forgotten contract.
.y offer and put in your notice today."

.ld he jump back to business as usual just like
had no cognitive thinking happening right now.
.g inside of her jumbled up mind made any sense. "I
.J to go."

She spun and almost ran, throwing open the office door and pushing her way around construction workers and delivery personnel and sous chefs. Her hands shook so badly that she could barely get her car door unlocked, but finally threw it open and slid onto the seat. She tossed the contract onto the seat next to her and rested her forehead against the steering wheel. Finally, she allowed herself to give into the impulse and put three shaking fingers against her trembling lips.

CHAPTER ELEVEN

Tony arrived at Robin's apartment at seven o'clock on the dot. A kind of nervous little excitement about a real dinner date with Robin made his smile stick and added a lightness to his step. He wanted to shower her with pretty things. She had so little pretty in her life. He ran his hand down the outside of his suit pocket and felt the bulge of Robin's promotion present. She would resist this gift, he knew, but he also knew she would eventually accept it.

He could hear loud music coming through the door. He paused to make sure he hadn't gone up an extra floor perhaps to stand at the wrong apartment door before rapping his knuckles hard on the door. No answer. He recognized the song and realized it neared the end so he waited. As soon as he heard a lull in the music between that song and the next, he knocked hard again. He heard "Come in!" just before he heard the beginning strands of the next song.

As he opened the door, the strong smell of oil paint

assailed his nostrils. With the couch and chair pushed out of the way, Maxine had a painter's canvas set up in front of the television. Music blared out of speakers from somewhere in the room. She wore a pair of torn jeans, a half-cropped T-shirt, and had her hair bundled on top of her head. In one hand she held a palette of paints, in the other, her paintbrush.

"Hi Tony," Maxine said. She waved her brush like a wand, gesturing with it while she spoke.

Tony walked in until he stood behind her. On the canvas in front of him lay an almost complete bird's eye view of Boston Harbor as one would suppose it looked about two hundred years ago, every detail as perfect as he could imagine it. Majestic ships filled the harbor, horses and carriages lined the docks. Amazed, he watched as she dipped the brush in some blue and touched up the water.

The door opened and closed behind him. He could barely tear his eyes away from the perfection of the painting to see Sarah come into the apartment. She rolled her eyes and went to the stereo system and turned the volume way down. She paused next to Tony and looked at the painting. "Are you in love again?"

"Deeply," Maxine answered without hesitation. She arched her neck until their heads touched before she went back to work. "Can you fix me a drink?"

"Sure. What do you want?"

"Something cold."

Sarah had to climb over the couch to get to the kitchen, and Tony smiled while he continued to watch Maxine paint. Her brush moved with absolute confidence as she touched up here and there, fixing things he didn't realize were imperfect until she perfected them. Finally, she set the palette and brush down and stepped back to stand next to him. "What do you think?"

"I think you're a genius."

She laughed as she took a paint splattered rag and started rubbing at her stained fingers. "I've liked you from the first, Tony."

"Have you ever had a showing?"

"Nah. I don't do it for that. I just do it." She grinned up at him. "In my heart, I'm an advertiser. This is just dabbling. A hobby, really."

"This is the best dabbling I've ever seen. If you change your mind, let me know. I own a couple of studios around the country."

She shrugged and rushed over to get the drinks from Sarah's hands so that she could climb back over the couch.

"I'm serious, Maxine."

"I can tell," she said, "but I have no desire to make this my profession. I already have a profession."

He stared at the canvas again. The colors, the details, looked so perfect that the painting immediately swept him back in time. He could almost taste the salt air and hear the sounds from the dock. "No reason why you can't do both."

She handed him a glass of ice water. He accepted the drink and Maxine said, "Dozens of reasons, actually. But let's just leave it alone for now. You can bring it up again when I've not just come out of a massive all-night painting session."

Sarah sat down in the chair sideways, leaning against one arm and throwing her legs over the other. "Who is it? Donald?"

Maxine started packing her paints. "Donald? Who?" Then she stopped and threw her head back, laughing hard. "No, honey, Dwayne."

At Tony's confused look, Sarah grinned. "Maxine only paints when she's in love."

She snapped the case shut with a click. "He proposed to me last night."

Sarah raised an eyebrow. "Are you getting married?"

"Of course not. It was fun to get asked."

Tony said, "If you're in love, why say no?"

She reached up and released the clip securing her hair, shaking the black tendrils loose from their confinement. "Because, this is only fun love. It will fade." She stared at him, her green eyes serious. "I'm waiting for the big one. The real deal."

Sarah rolled her eyes and stood. "The big one?"

Maxine stared at Tony while she spoke, making him aware that she understood the warmth in his eyes meant for her older sister alone. "The real one. The one that is destined. The one that will last forever."

"How will you know the difference?" Sarah chided.

Though her sister spoke, she never took her eyes off Tony. "Oh, some people just know. Others need to be shown. Right, Tony?"

He gave a barely perceptible nod of his head, but his smile stretched wide and real across his face.

Maxine climbed onto the couch and drew her legs up to her chin. "Where are you going tonight?" Maxine asked.

"Harbor House," Tony confided.

"Wow." She pushed herself up. "Hey, Robin!" She yelled, angling her head toward the hallway. "Scratch that black dress and get the blue one out of my closet. With the scarf."

Robin's voice came from behind a closed door. "What blue dress with the scarf?"

"It's in a bag in the closet." Maxine crossed her hands behind her head. "Don't forget the shoes," she said loudly. "They're in the Piedmont's box."

She turned her head to grin at Tony before she closed her eyes and smiled. "I have this big salary and nothing to spend it on, so I'm afraid that I've become a clothes hound."

"Why don't you guys move into a bigger apartment?"

"Sure, as soon as you convince my darling sister that I'm done having things and I am perfectly capable of contributing to the household."

"What do you mean?"

"She wants me to move, but she won't move with me. I deserve nice things, she says." She lay her head back against the couch and closed her eyes. "Makes me angry. That girl saved me, literally and figuratively. Saved my life from any number of horrors and repeats of horrors, and she expects me just to leave her in this rat hole and move because I make a good salary." She raised her head to look at him. "In two more years, Sarah gets out of school. Maybe I can get her to relax a little then."

"How many dresses in bags do you have?" Robin's voice was muffled, but irritated just the same. "Geeze, Maxi!"

Maxine sighed then pushed herself to her feet. "I'll go rescue my wardrobe." She jumped over the couch. "Make yourself at home. I have to talk her into the shoes, too."

Tony chuckled. "Take your time."

He made a quick phone call and pushed his reservation back by thirty minutes. He stood in the cramped living room, touched his fingers to his tie to make sure the knot was still in place, and felt the gift in his pocket again.

In his peripheral vision, he saw Sarah stand and sling her backpack over her shoulder. He turned to fully face her.

"I have to get to my parents' house. We're having a planning meeting tonight for our church's fall festival."

Tony's interested was peaked. "What church?"

"Crescent Christian in Framingham."

Mentally shifting through names and faces and people and places, he finally identified Crescent. "I know that church. Isn't Dr. Skinner the senior pastor there?"

"He is now, but he's retiring soon. There is already some uproar about staffing and such going on."

Tony nodded. "People don't like change." He slipped his hands in his pockets and his fingertips ran over Robin's gift. "Tell me about this festival."

"We have games and candy and blow up toys where kids can bounce and play. We serve hot dogs and chili and popcorn. It's a lot of fun. Tons of kids from the neighborhood come who would never have come to the church for another reason."

"We do something very similar. I go to Boston Central Christian. I've never served on the planning committee, but I'm often approached about donations and sponsorships. Let me know if there's anything you need in the way of anything like that." He pulled a business card from an inner pocket. From his shirt pocket, he extracted a gold pen and wrote on the back of the card. "This is my secretary's name and direct extension. She knows your name. Just let her know anything you need. Any gaps we can fill."

Sarah took the card. "I have to admit; I'm feeling a little intimidated and overwhelmed at the same time. "Your secretary knows my name?"

Tony smiled and shrugged. "Sure. You're Robin's sister."

"We struggle financially every year to put on the festival. To think that this year, the potential release of the financial burden…" she stopped speaking as tears filled her eyes and her face flooded with a red flush. "I don't know what to say."

Tony smiled, trying to put her at ease. "There's no reason to say anything. We're all working for one goal, are we not?"

Sarah sniffled. "I wish everyone I had to work with thought the same way you do." She shifted her glasses on her face and quickly swiped at her eyes. "How does Robin handle your faith?"

His laugh barked through the room. "With blinders. If she doesn't mention it, then it doesn't affect her, I think." His face turned serious. "I pray for her, constantly, though."

Sarah opened her mouth then closed it. She closed her eyes, huffed out a breath, and spoke quickly. "Listen, I've known her for a long time. She isn't open to the Word."

"She wouldn't be from you."

Her eyes widened. "Why not?"

"Because in her mind, she is responsible for you. She is the eldest, the protector, the provider." He smiled just to soften the next sentence, for him and for her. "She's already been in hell, so what can you possibly teach her?"

Leaning against the arm of the couch, Sarah shrugged and nodded again. "I know. Even Christ was rejected by his own people. I've at least tried to serve as a silent witness for Robin and Maxi, but I don't think I've ever done any good."

"While on this earth, we'll never see all of the fruits of our labors. You've planted seeds. Between your seed and my..." He almost said his love for her sister, but stopped short. When he confessed his love for Robin, he would do it while looking into her amazing sapphire eyes, not while talking to her little sister in a cramped living room. "... and my not so silent witness, we can only pray that those seeds will grow and root and bloom and eventually thrive."

Sarah's pocket buzzed and she pulled out a phone, quickly scanning the text message that had just come in. "I'm going to be late. I enjoyed talking to you, Tony. I hope we get a chance to talk when we don't each already have other plans."

He smiled, wanting to hug her. His brotherly feelings for her didn't surprise him in the slightest. "I look forward to it."

After Sarah left, he turned back to the painting to study it further, in awe of the detail and the beauty. Maxine had surprised him, and he enjoyed that. He took in the painting and searched it with a sense of discovery and near excitement. Tony often felt at least one step ahead of everyone. He endured—and invented new ways to cope with—the boredom suffered by the brilliant every single day. He found most of life, and most people he encountered, extremely predictable. Maxine proved unpredictable. He liked that.

Time passed, but he didn't mind the wait. There was no reason to hurry. He sipped his water and considered the painting, trying to see all of the hidden elements.

"Hi."

He turned, stopping short when he saw Robin.

"Wow." He managed.

Her dress—a long blue sheath that fell tightly from her breasts to the floor—had a slit on one leg that reached to her knee and two thin spaghetti straps at the shoulders. It molded her curves beautifully, showed the faintest hint of cleavage, and accented the flare of her hips. She hadn't put her hair up for once, and it cascaded halfway down her back.

"You look amazing." Tony expressed sincerely after a thorough appraisal.

Her cheeks fused with color. "Thank you." She held up the thin wisp of material that served as the scarf. "What do I do with this?"

"Well," he said, reaching into his pocket with one hand while he took the scarf from her and stepped behind her. "What some do is drape it around their necks and let the ends trail behind them." He pulled the necklace out of his pocket and slipped it around her neck before she knew what he was doing. "When you wear jewelry, though, it's fine just to drape it over one arm."

She gasped as her hand flew up to her neck. "What did—" Her fingers traced the sapphires, feeling the shape of the dripping gems, brushing over the rough diamonds, feeling the weight of actual stones against her skin. She didn't turn around. Instead, she skipped to the mirror hanging next to the door and gasped again at the sight.

"Tony, I don't want—"

He followed her until he stood behind her and tenderly laid his fingertips on her bare shoulders. His eyes met hers in the mirror. "Shush! It's perfect for the dress."

She stared at him, feeling a mixture of excitement and anger. Her hand never left the necklace. "I don't want jewelry from you, Tony. That's not why I'm with you."

"I believe you. I remember how you returned my tip." He grinned in genuine pleasure and his eyes twinkled with mischief. "Ironically, it only makes me even more inclined to give you expensive gifts." His fingers moved softly up and down her arms. "I bought it a few days ago because the blue sapphires were a near perfect match with your eyes."

His fingers sent shivers through her whole body, but she slowly shook her head. "No. I'm not the type to shower with expensive gifts. Please, I don't want—"

He turned her around so that he could look directly at her. He slid an arm around her lower back, pulling her gently to him. "Just for tonight." His lips gently brushed hers. "We're celebrating in style because you deserve it."

Robin's lips tingled and she wanted to step forward and ask him to kiss her again. Kiss her deeper, longer. This close to him, feeling the heat from his body and smelling the amazing tang of his aftershave, she felt safe, secure, important. The warmth of his eyes beckoned her to let him give her this necklace, and she relented because, for some reason, pleasing him was important to her.

"Okay." She ran her hands over the length of it, until she felt the clasp in the back, terrified it wasn't secured properly and she'd lose what surely cost a few semesters worth of medical books. "Okay, but just this one time."

Tony ran a hand down her arm until he could clasp her fingers with his and bring her hand up to his mouth. He brushed his lips over her knuckles. "Thank you, *cara*. You make that necklace look beautiful. Shall we go?"

You know, I applied here before Benedicts'." Robin took a sip of her water then propped her chin in her hand. "Almost got the job, too." In the dim light of the restaurant, with the candlelight flickering on their table, she felt very alone with him. In the intimate setting, other couples at other tables obviously felt it, too, because people spoke quietly, almost in hushed tones, keeping up the secluded facade.

"Oh? What happened?"

"The manager objected to the fact that I wouldn't sleep with him."

"Really?" His voice was very calm, very cool, and his eyes glittering and very hard. "Pray tell, which manager was that?"

She felt a chill run up her back, glad that she wasn't the object of his anger. "Umm, his name was Brad, I think. No. No, wait, it was Brian."

He relaxed almost visibly. "I see. I fired him years ago."

"You?" She laughed. Not because he fired someone. She often feared losing one or both of her jobs and having nothing. She laughed because of the casual way he just dismissed it. "Of course. Why wouldn't I think that you owned this, too?"

His smile was quick and his eyes looked almost warm again. "I own a lot of things." He quickly reached out and took her hand. "I'm very happy that you're going to take the job."

She decided to speak in a straightforward with him again. She saw no sense in pretenses. "What happens when we—" she let the sentence hang in the air, confident that he would know what she asked.

He laced their fingers and looked at their joined hands. He liked the contrasts. Her hand light, his dark. Hers small and delicate, his bigger and stronger. "What happens when we break up and have all of this anger and angst and you still work for me?"

She couldn't help smiling at his choice of wording. "Yeah. Something like that."

"I don't know. I have zero experience with this. All I know is that I want to spend time with you. I want you to want to spend time with me. You're also the perfect person to manage Hank's. There has to be a way to do it all."

Robin shook her head. "I haven't signed the contract yet. Maybe—"

Tony squeezed her hand. "Listen. I really like you, and I respect you so much for everything you've done in your life. Whether or not we're involved romantically isn't going to change that."

She sat back while the waiter arrived with their first course. As he set the bowls of French onion soup in front of them, Robin watched Tony. He was sincere, she thought. He wasn't the type to play games. She picked up her spoon as the waiter departed, and felt excitement building. She hoped that they could work together once they fell apart. All she knew right now was that she wanted to spend this time with Tony and she really wanted to manage Hank's.

"Besides," Tony said, "I believe God brought us together for a purpose. I don't see anger and angst involved in fulfilling God's desires.' He winked and held out his hand. "Shall we bless our meal?"

Robin set her spoon back down and took his hand.

CHAPTER TWELVE

Rain pummeled the city for weeks, a cold rain that drove people indoors and off the streets while autumn surrendered to winter. Thanksgiving passed and the rain turned into sleet, which then turned into ice and snow.

The city buildings looked even more gray, morphing to match the dirty slush lining the roads. Even though the sun hadn't shown in weeks and the cold gray world remained perpetually wet, Robin's spirits remained high.

She understood now, what Maxine had meant when she said that she'd simply felt happier and not happy. Robin looked forward to the next new day for the first time in her life. She looked forward to it with a smile and a sense of anticipation.

After giving Benedicts' notice, Robin took over for Hank as if the place belonged to her. The staff never felt the bump in the transition, and never once challenged her authority. She had worked as a bartender and a waitress for years. Despite the grueling aspect of maintaining two physically stressful jobs, neither one of them challenged her. Managing Hank's challenged every part of her—intellectually, emotionally, physically—and she woke each morning anticipating what new challenges would face her that day.

Viscolli Enterprises sent in a tutor to teach her the fundamentals of accounting. She fell in love with perfect columns of numbers on a spreadsheet, with balance sheets and figures and projections. She spent hours after hours working with the accounting team to streamline the archaic records keeping of Hank's from handwritten ledgers to a state-of-the-art computer system that linked her to the Viscolli empire. As she worked, she learned and learned, and soaked up everything that she could from the team of accountants and computer experts.

Hank's wife had served as his assistant manager, so she had a hole to fill with both of them suddenly leaving. After learning how to read a resume, then reading what felt like an endless stream of resumes, she finally settled on the current head hostess, Kelly Addison. Robin felt like, most importantly, that she could trust Kelly and that they could work together. The thirty-seven-year-old Navy wife and mother of three teenagers had not applied for the position but readily, and tearfully, accepted the offer. Then Robin had to go back to the resumes to find a new host or hostess.

Every turn in the bed, every new hour of every single day, brought something new and exciting to her life, and she realized that she loved her job.

Her little office in the back of the restaurant gradually became "hers" and not "Hank's". She no longer paused at the door with a hand raised to knock, and instead went through the threshold to her own inner sanctuary. Thanks to Maxine, photographs of her sisters showed up in pretty frames around the previously Spartan room. Then, thanks to Sarah, plants filled empty spots on shelves and the small window ledge. Her contributions included tins of peppermints, books on management and accounting, scattered coffee cups. Inside the walls of the little room, she could breathe, take a moment before charging back out into the challenge of managing Hank's.

Robin also discovered sleep. What a phenomenon. She slept six or even eight hours a night, now. Between two full-time jobs and the nightmares, good, restful sleep had become something of a luxury. Now, she left work as the restaurant closed, slept until late morning, and returned again as the lunch hour started.

Per company policy, she took two days off a week. Managers could work as many hours as required five days a week, but Viscolli Enterprises demanded without exception that managers take off Sundays and one other day of the week. She resisted. Tony threatened to fire her. She'd already quit Benedicts'. She capitulated.

She went to work early Mondays to do paperwork and place orders in the silence of the closed restaurant and worked until closing. Mondays had become her favorite day of the week. Typically, she took Wednesdays off. Wednesdays had a lighter customer load than any other day. She had always enjoyed having Sundays off, but adding an extra day of rest to her schedule threw her for a loop. She probably would have found herself climbing the walls of her apartment if she didn't always have looking forward to seeing Tony high on her list.

Despite the fact that he constantly worked out of town,

acquiring this or merging that, Tony called her every morning. She found that she looked forward to his calls, anticipated them. She would lie in bed, relaxed, rested, half a smile on her face and wait for the phone to ring.

He almost always showed up on Wednesday to spend the day with her. He would call the office on Tuesday afternoon and confirm plans for this movie or that museum or this lunch. They started holding hands as they walked. He would put his arm around her at the movie. He would kiss her, oh how he would kiss her, hello and good-bye and times and times in between.

The more time they spent together, the more relaxed he became about touching her. He would brush her hair from her face, run a hand down her arm, rub her neck. However, despite her request that night so many weeks ago in that dirty laundry room, Tony never took anything any further than casual touching, warm hugs, or tender kisses. Robin thought that maybe, instinctively, she could feel him holding something back. It confused her to think that as warm and—loving—as he acted, he hadn't really given her everything. Thinking that maybe his faith had something to do with it, she wondered why he agreed to her request the night of his birthday in the first place. Regardless, she didn't feel like she could approach the subject with anything less than mortification, so she left it alone and decided to wait and see what came next.

No longer did she anticipate him using her—or her using him—and then discarding her. She began to feel very special. She felt very important to him. Treasured. She thought of him now as her "boyfriend" and smiled the first time she used that term.

Lying in bed early Monday morning after Thanksgiving,

exhausted, sore, worn out from the last few weeks preparing for the holiday season, waiting for the phone to ring, she smiled. Contentment, happiness, and anticipation all waged a happy war inside of her. As she investigated these feelings, she detected a small frown mar her brow. Inside her heart, she felt like she had missed something—she didn't know what, but something—important.

She pondered that for a moment. Monday mornings were typically reflective, because Sunday had remained the one day she didn't get to spend with Tony or speak with Tony. Typically, church took up his entire day. It finally occurred to her that she missed him.

The more time she spent with him, the more she wanted to spend all of her free time with him. The thought of sitting next to him on a church pew, eating lunch after church with him and his friends, spending the entire day with him on the day he assigned such importance, held tremendous appeal to her. She decided that this coming Wednesday, she would go to his evening worship with him. He asked her every Wednesday and every Sunday if she wanted to go, and she always turned him down. Thinking about how much it would please him when she finally agreed to accompany him made her happy.

The phone interrupted her reverie. She snatched it up very quickly, not wanting it to wake her sisters. The caller ID confirmed Tony as the caller, so she simply said, "Good morning," with a smile on her face.

"Good morning, *cara*. How did you sleep?"

"Deeply. It's been an exhausting week."

"I imagine. It will stay that way until after New Year's."

"I know. Just working with the books I could see the

massive incline for December."

Tony paused before continuing. "I know you're tired, and since it's Monday you likely plan on getting to work early, but I was wondering if you could meet me for breakfast."

Excited little butterflies started dancing in her stomach as they always did in anticipation of seeing Tony. "Sure. Where?"

"I've had a couple of overseas phone calls this morning, so I'm already at my office. Do you mind coming here? We could have the hotel restaurant bring something up."

Considering the time, she made some mental calculations. "I'll probably take the Charlie. I imagine traffic is a chore right now. Give me about an hour and I should be there."

"*Aspetto*. I look forward to it. I can send a car if you wish."

"No. Don't be silly. Then we'd have to battle traffic both ways."

She could hear someone murmuring to him, but couldn't make out anything specific. "I have to go *cara*. I'll see you when you get here."

Robin threw the covers off of the bed and dashed to the closet to dress quickly so that she could get to the train.

Tony waited for Robin with a nervous anticipation he hadn't felt in a while. He couldn't predict the outcome of this conversation, and he didn't like that. His entire future stood in anticipation of how Robin would react.

As he ordered breakfast and waited for her, he thought back to the conversation he and Barry had the Wednesday before Thanksgiving...

"Did you lose track of time or something?"

Tony glanced up from his computer monitor and watched Barry saunter into the room. "Not lately." He saved his work and leaned his chair back. "Why do you ask?"

Barry sprawled into a chair across from the desk. "It's just odd that the high today is going to be a shivering twenty-nine, Christmas is just a month away, and no major deals that you're working on have crossed my desk. Despite all that, your plane hasn't left for Florida yet this year." He examined his nails.

"Really?"

"I also keep hearing rumors that the completely social Tony Viscolli has suddenly dropped from sight, which you only do when you're working on something major."

Tony leaned back in his chair. "Is that so?"

"Either you've suddenly decided you prefer the solitary life and you don't mind the cold so much, or you have a new lawyer and haven't told me. If you have a new lawyer, Tony, that would—you know—hurt my feelings."

"Well, I haven't found a new lawyer. No one submits billable hours like you do, Bear."

Barry laughed through his nose and half smiled. "You decided to live a life of solitude, then?"

Tony raised an eyebrow. "There's another possibility that might be keeping me here."

"Nothing has ever kept you here when the temperature

drops below fifty."

He opened his top drawer and pulled out the jewelry box, and without a word, tossed it to Barry. The former NFL star caught it with one massive hand and flipped open the lid with his thumb, exposing the ring with the square cut sapphire surrounded by diamonds. He shut the lid with a little pop, then opened it again for a closer look, his eyebrows knitting.

"Tony, this looks an awful lot like an engagement ring."

"Is that what it looks like?" Tony put his hands behind his head and leaned his chair even farther back. He felt a silly grin spread across his face.

"I don't know what to say. I mean, I know we've been friends for a long time, but this is just so sudden and unexpected." He started laughing. Without warning, he flipped the lid shut and tossed it back to Tony. "Can I have some time to think about it? What will my wife say?"

"Ha ha. Oh, so funny." He caught the box with one hand and tossed it on the top of his desk.

"That's pretty serious, man. I'm assuming you're still seeing Robin? That this ring is intended for her?"

"*Esatto*. Yes."

"Let me get this straight." He hooked his leg over his knee. "You're going to ask a girl to marry you who you didn't even meet until September? This past September. Barely three months ago."

"That's the plan." Tony could practically see the gears shifting in Barry's mind.

"I don't like it."

He smiled. "Jealousy doesn't suit you, Bartholomew."

Barry dropped the whole relaxed facade and leaned forward. "No, listen to me, Tony. It doesn't make sense. How do you know she's sincere? I mean, come on, what are you worth?"

Tony laughed. "You'd have to know Robin to know how absurd that sounds."

"That's the point, man. I'm your best friend and I have never interacted with her. Ever. Is she keeping you from your friends so that she can fully sink in the hooks?"

Tony's smile faded. "No, actually, I've been all over the map lately, and only manage to see her one day a week. I took her by the church and we had dinner with Peter and Caroline. Other than that, I've been keeping her from my friends so I don't have to share."

Barry nodded faintly. "That just adds to it. You've declined every holiday party you've been invited to, and I am fully aware of how much business you actually manage to conduct at those parties."

Tony sighed and rubbed his eyes. "Barry, how long have we known each other?"

Barry chuckled and fed Tony his own words from a few months ago. "Too long for you to even ask that question."

"You ever know me to make a bad decision? Have you ever known me to go into any situation without prayer and petition?"

Barry shrugged, "Not when it comes to business. This is not business."

Tony nodded and then pursed his lips. Diplomatically, Tony said, "I appreciate your concern as a friend, then. I honestly do."

"Is she saved?"

Tony froze and slowly stretched his hand to the gold pen lying on the blotter. He gently started to spin it. "Why?"

"Should I take that as a no, or continue to press for the answer?"

Closing his eyes, he felt a weariness settle on his shoulders that he hadn't felt in a couple of decades. "I pray for her every single day. Every minute of every day. It's the one reason that ring is in that box instead of on her finger." He opened his eyes again and stared hard at his friend.

Barry folded his hands together and laid them on the desk. "Tony…"

"There isn't a single thing you can say to me that I don't already know. I know that God doesn't desire for us to be unevenly yoked. I know that my feelings for her can be a tool Satan can use against me. I know that every time I'm alone with her I face temptation on a level so high that I don't know if I can fight another day without her prayer and consideration. I know all of that."

Tony started spinning the pen again. "I also know that the moment that I saw her, I felt drawn to her. I know that every moment in her presence fills me with encouragement, unfathomable joy, delight. I knew—I KNEW—that I was in love with her within a matter of days. Maybe I've known it my whole life. I believe, strongly, that she will love the Lord as much as I do. All I can do is stay faithful, pray for her, and just continue to be me."

Barry sat back again. Silence hung in the air for ten seconds, then for twenty. Finally, he said, "How does she feel about you?"

Tony rubbed both of his eyes and leaned back in his chair. "I don't know." He smiled and the seriousness left his face. "Well, actually, I know that she's in love with me. She just doesn't know that she knows it yet."

"Tony." He said the word on a sigh, and nothing else followed.

"I know that God is in control, *il mio amico*. I trust Him. I know you're afraid that I'm moving too fast, but I will not take this relationship any further as long as she is unsaved. I think there are few books I've read more in the last four months than the second book of Corinthians. In the sixth chapter, God is quite clear about this specific matter of the heart."

Barry sighed a deep rumbling sigh. He closed his eyes, took a couple of deep breaths, then opened them again. "I'd like to pray for you right now."

Tony coughed and cleared his throat against the emotions that flooded him. "I'd appreciate that very much." He stood and moved around the desk so that he could sit in the chair flanking Barry's. They turned their chairs facing each other and clasped hands and bowed their heads.

They had prayed for each other, jointly petitioning God for guidance and strength, and Tony felt his heart both lifted and burdened. The brotherly love that Barry displayed for him, the solidarity of his spiritual brother's love for him lifted and strengthened him in a way he hadn't realized he needed until the heaviness and imagined loneliness vanished before they said "Amen." The burden he felt to bring Robin to an acceptance of the truth sharpened in those whispered moments and became a near physical ache.

Tony had thought about that conversation and those shared moments of fellowship for the last few days. When he had invited Robin to attend services with him Sunday, he had prayed for God to convict her of the sincerity of the invitation. He had prayed that God could fill him with a visible light that would shine brightly through him and cover her. He had also prayed for revelation as he studied God's holy word.

All of it had culminated in his telephone call early this Monday morning. He didn't look forward to the conversation he knew he would need to have with Robin this morning, but he knew that he had to say what needed saying and he could not let it go unsaid even one more day.

His secretary announced Robin's arrival and it brought Tony fully back to the present. He took a deep calming breath and smiled as the door to his office opened. He strode forward, his hands outstretched, to greet her.

After a lingering welcoming kiss, Tony led Robin to the conference table and held the chair out for her. He had the conference table in his office set beautifully. A vase full of flowers matched the linen, china plates with the gold scrolling "V" logo of Viscolli Enterprises sat perfectly centered on linen place mats, a silver pot of coffee gleamed under the lights and a frosty carafe of orange juice sweated in the warmth of the room. A room service cart sat next to the table supporting an array of silver-dome covered dishes.

She took the proffered chair and he poured them both coffee. Then he lifted the dome lids on the room service cart, revealing muffins, bagels, corned beef, scrambled eggs, and a bowl of fresh fruit. Robin chose a bagel and some strawberries and couldn't help noticing that Tony took nothing for himself.

"You're not hungry?" She asked as she spread cream cheese on her whole-wheat bagel.

"I've been up for several hours and have already eaten." He waved his hand dismissively. "Enjoy. I'll just have coffee."

Robin tried to engage him in general idle talk while she ate, but he didn't respond with enthusiasm, his thoughts clearly elsewhere. Finally, she brushed the crumbs off of her fingertips and picked up her coffee cup. "What's up? Why the impromptu meeting?"

Tony always seemed so sure of himself. In the time that she'd known him, he never missed a beat. He always appeared to know what to say, how to say it, what to do and how to do it. She watched as he lifted his cup and set it down, as he rubbed a finger across his eye as if to ward off a headache, how he drummed his fingers on the table and realized he didn't know what to say or how to say it. She began to feel the beginnings of some pretty serious nerves dance along the back of her spine.

She cleared her throat. "I've always preferred a direct approach myself."

His eyes flashed surprised before he half grinned. "I appreciate you, Robin." As his fingers toyed with the knot on his tie, the diamond on his pinkie winked in the light. "I missed you yesterday. A lot." She opened her mouth to agree with him, but he held a finger up. "My worship is a huge part of my life. It encourages me, inspires me, rejuvenates me, and feeds my spirit. I cannot imagine getting through the kind of weeks I have without devoting an entire day to God and discovering the accompanying peace and solace I find in Him. I also find myself distracted by missing you. Frankly, it's getting to be a problem for me, and it's interfering with my worship."

"Tony, that's something I've been wanting to talk with you about as well."

Thrown off of his prepared speech, he cocked his head. "Oh?"

She smiled. "There's this strange appeal to the thought of experiencing your church with you. I don't know why, but I do want to go. I'd already decided that on Wednesday when you ask me to go, I would say yes."

Tony closed his eyes, relief flooding from his heart through his soul and whispered a thank you to God, *"Ti ringrazio, Dio."* He opened them again, and reached for her hand, cupping it with both of his. "I am so very happy to hear that." He smiled, and the smile warmed his eyes, giving her heart a little extra beat to it. "I planned on giving you an ultimatum."

Robin's eyes widened. "Wow. Good timing on my part."

Tony brought her hand to his lips and kissed the knuckles. "I don't know if I was going to be able to go through with it, but yes, *cara*. Excellent timing. Thank you so much for preempting what might have been a bad move on my part."

This time, Robin sat forward and used her other hand to cup one of his. "I am a straight forward kind of girl, Tony. I don't pick up on a lot of hints or subtleties, and I'll drive myself crazy wondering what you mean or what you feel if you don't come out and tell me."

Tony wondered if she realized how much she had changed over the last few months. She had completely blossomed with confidence and strength that he knew for certain she doubted ever even existed in her. "So you're saying just be blunt and straightforward?" Oh, the things he wished he could tell her. How much he loved her, how much he desired to make her his wife, how he longed for her soul to know salvation, for her to give her life to Christ. Despite what she said, though, he knew she wasn't ready to hear it.

"Yes. Please just tell me what's up. I work much better that way."

He leaned forward and brushed his lips over hers. How much longer must he contain this amazing joy he had in the love he felt for her? "*Cara*, there is a time for everything under heaven. I hope to tell you everything in time. I assure you I will try to be blunt and straightforward when the time comes."

CHAPTER THIRTEEN

Robin watched the clock all day. She felt a little nervous energy in her stomach about going to church that night with Tony. What did one do at church? Would the people act weird? Would she act weird? She hoped she didn't embarrass herself, or worse yet, embarrass Tony.

These thoughts plagued her off and on all day, so she went to work to try to take her mind off of it. It didn't help. The unknown kept distracting her from her job. She tried to work accounting, but couldn't focus. She tried to get with Casey about orders, but he had spent the morning fighting with a vegetable supplier and she couldn't bother him. Finally, she decided to just walk through the front of the house, check on customers, check on the hostess and the wait staff.

When she met Peter and Caroline, Robin thought that their loving acceptance of her fell well outside of the norm, an exception to every rule of life and living she had ever learned. Never before had anyone treated her so kindly, so naturally, without any expectations. When she walked into the doorway of the main church building of Boston Central Christian Church on that Wednesday night, though, she felt like she'd walked into the open arms of long lost family.

They came together and sang songs. A guitarist and someone playing a tambourine provided the only accompaniment, and the lyrics appeared on a big screen behind them. Robin enjoyed the songs, enjoyed the emotion and the passion behind them. She enjoyed hearing Tony's voice as he sang next to her. She found herself clapping along or smiling or doing both at the same time.

After songs and prayer, they broke away into smaller groups. Robin found herself in a classroom sitting on a folding metal chair, a Styrofoam cup of coffee in one hand a worksheet in the other, and the Bible Tony had given to her as a gift after they pulled into the church parking lot that evening sitting on her lap crisp and new. While holding the worksheet, she laid her hand on top of the Bible so that the back of her hand lay against the dark blue leather, enjoying the cool feel of it against her skin and instinctively knowing that this gift meant more to Tony than the dark blue sapphire necklace ever could.

As Tony took the seat next to her, he spoke softly to her, "There are several classes we could attend. This one is studying the book of Daniel. The teacher used to be a rabbi before he came to know Christ, and his Old Testament insight is amazing."

None of that meant anything to Robin. She didn't know what he meant by the book of Daniel. She didn't know what the phrase "came to know Christ" meant, though she thought perhaps it had something to do with the conversation Tony had with her about getting off of the street, and she had absolutely no idea what Old Testament meant. The teacher started speaking, though, so she didn't ask for clarification.

Everyone in the class showed genuine pleasure at meeting Robin. She felt so loved and accepted that she hoped the class would never end. The teaching mostly went over her head, because she had zero background in anything to do with the Bible or church and with the way the discussions moved, she assumed she sat in an advanced class. She didn't mind and found herself almost sorry when it ended.

People bombarded Tony as they left the class and made their way out of the church. She quit counting how many people asked to meet with him for this or that, how many wanted this lunch appointment or that coffee date. Many came to just meet her with kindness in their eyes and a hug or a warm handshake to hand out.

After church services, she found herself back down that row of little houses with the picket fences and inside a different house—this time, the home of the former rabbi, Abram Rabinovich. He was probably about fifty, several inches shorter than her, with almost no hair. He had a stunning wife, tall and thin with a beautiful face and strong Eastern European features.

"Sofia's family came from the Ukraine in the early seventies," Abram said as Sofia set a coffee tray on the low table in front of them then perched on the arm of his chair. "We met as children at synagogue so long ago that to find the exact date you might have to cut us in half and count the rings to be sure."

Sofia smiled as she draped her arm across her husband's shoulders and spoke with a slight accent. "We were married when we were seventeen. Twenty-nine beautiful years."

He laid a hand on her knee. "Not all of them so beautiful." He looked at Robin and Tony. "When Sofia came to know Christ, I'm afraid I didn't take it so well."

"Of course you didn't," Sofia said. "You had worked for fifteen years to get to where you were and were being offered that job at Brandeis University." She winked at Robin. "But you came around."

"Kicking and screaming," Abram said with a smile.

Robin shook her head. "I don't understand. If you were a rabbi, didn't you already 'know the Lord'?" She purposefully made air quotes so that he would know the clarification she sought.

Abram sat forward slightly and made a tent with his fingers. "I did not know Christ Jesus, God's only Son, to be my personal Lord and Savior. I studied God, but had no relationship with Christ."

"What's the difference?"

Abram pulled a pair of reading glasses out of his shirt pocket and held out his hand. "May I see your Bible?" As Robin handed it to him, he thanked her and flipped through a few pages. "This is a great version, and it has a comprehensive study guide. You are a smart girl. I can see that in your eyes. My suggestion to you is to read this book. When you read it, you'll understand the difference." He handed it back to her still open. She saw the words "The Gospel of Mark" in bold print across the top of the page.

"Start near the end?"

Sofia chuckled warmly. "No, darling. The Bible is not one book. It's like a library of books that are sorted by type. You have the law, which is in the front. You have prophets, poems, wisdom, eyewitnesses to Christ Jesus, letters, what our future will bring. You can read any book in any order you want. Start with Mark, it's a quick read and he talks all about what Jesus did. Then go to John. He was with Jesus, and saw the same things Mark spoke of, but used more words to describe them and focused a lot more on what Jesus said."

Robin nodded and thanked them. She looked over at Tony who sat next to her on the couch. "I imagine you've read this," she said with a smile.

He grinned and moved his hand from her shoulder to cup the back of her neck and squeeze. "A few times—and in a couple of different languages."

Sofia set her coffee cup on the table and stood. "Anyone interested in some cake? I don't cook, but I shop at wonderful bakeries."

They enjoyed the time at the Rabinovich's. Robin enjoyed watching them together. The love they had for each other shone through every gesture, every word, every touch. She liked watching their interactions and found herself scooting closer to Tony on the couch, and ended up cradled in his arm, holding his hand that draped over her shoulder, her arm resting against his leg. It felt comfortable and right to sit like this with him.

She wanted to freeze time and stay in that room in that little house for hours and hours more, but the clock ticked on and they had to leave. As Tony took her to her door that night, she wrapped her arms around his waist and hugged him to her, inhaling the smell of his cologne, enjoying the feel of the heat of his skin through his shirt. She didn't know how long they stood there, but when she finally broke the hug and stepped back slightly, he cradled her face in his hands and kissed her so sweetly, so gently that emotion flooded her system and clogged her throat. She had to blink tears away.

When he broke the kiss, she laid her head on his shoulder and stood there in the comfort of his arms. "Thank you for my Bible," she finally said, her lips nearly grazing the skin of his neck as she spoke.

"I'm glad you liked it. Did you enjoy church?" He asked.

"I did. I'm so glad I went." She sighed knowing that the night had to end. Straightening, she pulled her door key out of her purse. "I hope you'll be back from wherever in time to go again Sunday."

"If I was on the moon this week, I'd be back to take you to church on Sunday," he said. He pulled her close again and gave her one more long, lingering kiss.

Her arms slipped up around his neck and she kissed him back, feeling a flood of different emotions this time, less tender and sweet and more wanting, perhaps needing something—needing more. When he raised his head, he closed his eyes and rested his forehead against hers. "As it is," he said, his voice rough and low, "I'll be in town for the rest of the week. I'm really, really looking forward to church with you on Sunday."

"I am, too," she said. "Come inside."

She felt him tense as the words sank in, felt the muscles knot beneath her fingertips. She liked the feel of his strength. His voice sounded like a low growl as he asked, "Are your sisters home?"

She kissed his neck and felt his heat beneath her lips. Against his skin, she answered, "No."

He felt tight like a bowstring, tight like a fist, tight like a clenched jaw. She felt his pulse race in his neck and heard him take a massive breath before he said, "Then, let me just say no to your kind request. Understand that I genuinely appreciate the invitation. I hope you extend it again when the time is right."

"My sisters need to be home for you to come inside?"

"For now, yes." He said as if reminding himself.

"Is this a God thing?"

"It's about respecting you and respecting myself, *cara*. Respecting you as much as myself, actually. Kind of a golden rule thing."

It had never occurred to her that he respected her. What had she done to deserve his respect? He had slain dragons. She had simply scratched out a living for herself and her sisters. The mystery of the respect this man had for her would probably keep her puzzling for weeks.

Then he kissed her and her thoughts vanished. She had no idea how much time passed as they stood there in each other's arms, but eventually she found herself back in her apartment, alone, leaning against the door as she listened to the faint sound of his footsteps walking away. She could not hear the reluctance in his step, and had no idea of the very real battle he waged with his flesh to make himself continue to put one foot in front of the other. She ran her fingertips lightly over her lips, feeling them tingle at the memory of his kiss.

Her work week went quickly. Sunday morning arrived and Robin woke up excited, anxious to see Tony and anxious for church. As she dressed in a baby blue cashmere sweater and a tan suede skirt with knee-high boots, an outfit on loan to her from Maxine, she thought about the conversation with Abram and his talk about how knowing about God and a relationship with Jesus didn't mean the same thing. She pondered the love and generosity that poured from all of the people she had met at the church, all of Tony's friends and employees with whom she had interacted.

As she brushed her hair, she stared at her own reflection and pondered. If something tangible, something attainable, worked at the catalyst for the happiness and contentment she found in the people in Tony's realm; responsible for the way they appeared to rise above the selfishness of human nature that Robin had always known as the rule in humanity rather than the exception; then maybe she wanted to attain that tangible thing in her life, too. She wondered, though, how one went about acquiring this thing.

It seemed like it all centered around a personal relationship with Jesus Christ. Her entire experience with personal relationships existed in Maxine, Sarah, and now Tony. She had casual interactions with people at work, but only casual. She had never scoured the personals and never joined a dating service and she never missed dating because you don't miss what you don't have. She spent too many years working too hard and too long to leave room for anyone else in her life, so she didn't go to happy hours or parties or movies or anything with co-workers that might end in uncomfortable entanglements. It worked out when she became the manager because no friendships got in the way of her doing her job, but it also meant that she had very little skill in acquiring a personal relationship with anyone, deity or not.

Tony's arrival at her door broke through her thoughts and she quickly put her brush away and moved through the apartment. She opened the door and grinned, so happy to see him and to get to spend the day with him that she just wanted to laugh with joy.

Tony always had to prepare himself to see Robin, to steel himself as he waited for her to open the door. Her physical beauty had a lot to do with it—her face and her eyes simply took his breath away. He loved the shape of her body, he loved her height and how the few times she'd worn heels she stood at least an inch taller than him which forced him to look up into her eyes. Oh, how he loved the way she moved. More than any of that, though, he simply longed for her, for so much from her, that he had to shore himself up when he saw her lest he cave in to those longings.

He longed to touch her and hold her and kiss her. He longed to tell her how deeply he felt for her, how much he loved her and desired to have her at his side for eternity. He longed to see her commit to Christ and to love the Lord their God with all of her heart and all of her soul. He longed for so much from her that, occasionally, he felt relief that they couldn't see each other every single day or he feared he would eventually just give in to the pressures of his flesh and of his heart.

When Robin opened the door, he almost had to take a step back. She grabbed her coat and her purse and stepped out of her apartment. The light blue sweater she wore made her eyes positively glow; the blue in them so vivid he thought he might drown in those sapphire pools. More than that, though, something about her had changed. She radiated some sort of positive energy that he could not quite define but that tugged at him. She had a smile on her face that lit up the dim hallway and a laugh in her voice that struck musical tones.

Giving in, just for a moment, just for a small moment, he put his hand on the back of her neck and pulled her to him. His lips drank in the last of a laugh, and he felt it sparkle through his veins like a bubbly wine, leaving him drunk on her and wanting yet more. Rather than surrender all control and find himself just pushing her against the wall and ravishing her, he pulled back and away, putting his hands on her shoulders and physically taking a step back. He smiled at her, at the glow of joy on her face and the skirting of desire in her eyes. "You look beautiful, *cara. Bello*. I like the sweater."

Robin smiled. "Thank you. Maxine helped me."

"She has a good eye." He took her hand and held it as they walked down to his car.

Driving to the church, while they made small talk and enjoyed comfortable silences, she thought about that conversation she'd had with Tony in that dim laundry room those few months ago. How different things turned out than what she, without any thought about it at all, anticipated. She had expected sex, casual no-strings-attached sex, and then expected him to cast her away when he had no further use for her. Never—with the way that she had felt about him at the time—never would she have expected to count the minutes until she could see him again, to enjoy sitting next to him, to reach for his hand and hold it with hers, or to attend church with him. Whatever she might have imagined, the reality felt so much better, so amazing and wonderful that she wished she knew how to talk to God and thank Him properly for it.

As Tony pulled into the busy parking lot of the church, he felt Robin's hand clench in his and looked over at her.

She looked so content, so happy that he wanted to ask her about her thoughts, about whatever had changed inside of her. He hoped that she would realize it and initiate the conversation.

The air stung as they got out of the car and hurried into the church building. What Robin experienced Wednesday with the guitar and the tambourine did nothing to prepare her for Sunday morning and all its glory. A full orchestra had set up on the stage, hundreds of people milled about talking, laughing, looking for seats. Ushers ran back and forth, seating people, pushing wheelchairs, talking on radios. The big screen that had given the words to lyrics now flashed through announcements and news.

Robin and Tony found seats after speaking with dozens of people, some of whom she had met Wednesday. By the time they sat down, service began and, while she had enjoyed the music Wednesday night, Robin absolutely fell in love with the music Sunday morning. The orchestra played beautifully. The words all seemed to personally move her. The sound of almost a thousand voices raised in praise trembled through her soul.

After songs and songs and prayer and songs, the pastor approached the podium. He preached out of the book of John, a book that Robin had just started reading the morning before. He preached a sermon about love, redemption, and acceptance. He quoted the Bible and walked from one end of the platform to the other while energetically and passionately expressing how much God longed to have a personal relationship with each person in the building. He preached for forty minutes, and Robin felt every single word as if he spoke to her alone. As he stood there at the end of the platform and faced her section of the congregation, he raised his Bible in the air and said with such conviction that Robin felt the emotions closing up her throat, "God loves you and wants to know you. All you have to do," he paused and softened his voice and brought his hands to his chest, "all you have to do is let Him. Just open the door to your heart and let Him in."

As he turned around, the choir stood and quietly started singing. Enthralled, Robin listened to the words as the pastor moved along the platform and continued to speak. The choir sang, "Softly and tenderly Jesus is calling, calling for you and for me."

The pastor spoke over the song, "He's calling for you to come to Him!"

The choir continued, "See on the portals he's waiting and watching, watching for you and for me."

The pastor's voice rose above the music again. "All you have to do to bring Jesus into your heart is come forward. Come forward right now and accept that call from Jesus, that call to come home."

Robin felt an overwhelming emotion that took over every single cell in her body. It centered in her heart, over her chest, and spread out, magnifying by the second until she felt like something would physically burst out of her chest. She gripped the back of the chair in front of her and felt her knees start to tremble, and feared she'd fall.

The music grew a little louder and the choir sang a little stronger. "Come home, come home; ye who are weary come home."

"Are you weary?" She swore the pastor looked directly at her again.

The music poured through her very essence, the words wrote themselves on her heart. "Earnestly, tenderly, Jesus is calling, calling, O sinner, come home!"

"Come home." He held his hand out as if he looked beyond the rows and rows of filled pews and spoke directly to Robin, personally. "Come home."

Not even certain that her legs would carry her, Robin stepped out in the aisle. She didn't realize that Tony walked with her, his hand on the small of her back, but when she reached the front, an older woman with the kindest eyes she had ever encountered came forward to meet her.

She held both hands out and Robin placed hers in them. As soon as their skin touched, Robin fell to her knees, sobbing. "I'm so weary," she sobbed.

"I know." On her own knees, the woman put her arms around Robin's shoulders and wept with her. "I know, child."

With Tony kneeling beside her, his arm around her waist, Robin listened to the woman as she led her in prayer, taught her the words to say, how to say them, so that as she spoke the words, "Jesus, please forgive me of my sins and come into my heart," the pressure that had built and built inside of her chest during the sermon burst forth, like a million tiny sparks flooding from her chest through every vein in her body. It left her tingling, weak, and as it subsided, she felt strangely complete and fulfilled, and a peace settled over her shoulders like a mantle.

She didn't feel embarrassed about the storm of emotions that propelled her earlier as she thought she should. Instead, she looked at Tony and saw the joy in his eyes and felt elated. He helped her to her feet and after they each hugged the woman, they held hands as they walked back up the aisle to their seats.

Robin lifted the damp hair off of her neck and took a

few steadying breaths. She took the bulletin that she had placed inside of her Bible to mark the spot from where the pastor had preached and used it to fan her flushed face. Tony put his arm around her waist and pulled her to his side, cradling her next to him as they remained standing, singing the song that the choir had sung earlier, while more people flooded the front of the auditorium and sought their way home, too.

CHAPTER FOURTEEN

Robin propped her elbow on the kitchen table and rested her forehead in her hand. She stared at the calendar in front of her, with horror. Somehow, the week snuck up on her and here she sat, the morning of the night of Tony's mega Viscolli Corporate Christmas party. "What am I supposed to wear to something like that?"

Maxine groaned and stretched, graceful as a jungle cat and with just as much pent up energy. "I wish you'd mentioned this before the actual day of."

"Honestly, I was hoping that something would happen that would keep me from having to go."

"Like what?"

"I don't know. Flood? Meteor? Locusts? Terrorist attack?"

"Okay. Let me think." Maxine rubbed her forehead, wishing the sinus headache would quit interfering with her thoughts. "Ugh, my brain is not functioning this morning."

"I knew that live Christmas tree you bought would

mess with your allergies," Robin said with a touch of humor and a dose of concern.

"You enjoy saying, 'I told you so?'" She took a delicate sip of her orange juice. "It's in the back alley. Maybe a cat will use it as a scratching post or something more heinous."

"All I could find is Midol." Sarah came into the kitchen and set the bottle in front of Maxine, who sighed and popped open the tamper proof lid with one thumb.

"Well, my headache might not go away, but at least I won't have cramps."

"It has aspirin in it. Your headache will be taken care of."

"I was joking, Sarah. Sarcasm. Ever heard of it?"

"Only since I moved in here."

Robin groaned. "What is wrong with you two? You've been snapping at each other since yesterday morning."

Maxine stared at Sarah. "If you don't tell her, I will."

Sarah tore her eyes from Maxine's and stared at the table in front of her. "It's just that… um, I mean… well…."

Maxine swallowed two of the pills with her juice and slammed the glass down, wincing at the sharp sound. "What little sis here is trying to get out is that she isn't going down to Florida with us for Christmas."

The words cut straight to her heart. Hoping she could keep her expression under control, she glanced at Sarah. "Oh? Did something come up?"

Her sister refused to meet her eyes. "Well, it's just that mom and dad have never had Christmas without me. I mean, I know I've never been with you, either, but—"

Maxine tossed her hair over her shoulder. "Her mommy started crying."

Sarah gasped and looked up. "You are horrible."

"No, you are. Robin works so hard, and you're constantly putting your parents in front of her. That was great when you were fifteen or even seventeen. We were happy you didn't have to live our lives, then, but you're an adult now, Sarah, and you need to learn that your mother manipulates you to keep you right there by her side."

"That's not true!"

Maxine raised her voice. "You want to bet? The woman cried when her nineteen-year-old said she had the opportunity to fly down to Florida in a private jet and spend three days in a mansion on the beach."

"No! She's just worried about who…" Sarah gasped and jerked her eyes in Robin's direction.

The pain in her heart twisted like a knife. Oh, yes. What kind of element might the streetwise Robin and Maxine expose their precious Sarah to unchaperoned? The glow of a week of basking in the glory of God, in her newfound salvation, in her relationship with Tony started to dim. Robin put her hands over her ears. "Stop it! Both of you! I don't want to hear another word."

She stood slowly, feeling as if she had turned to glass and if she moved too fast she might shatter. "Sarah, spend Christmas wherever you want. It won't be the same without you, but it wouldn't be for your parents, either." She looked at Maxine. "Do you have plans for today? I think I've decided to buy a dress instead of borrowing one of yours, but I'll probably need you to help me pick one out."

Maxine glared at Sarah one more time then looked at her watch. "No, I can't. I have to get some work done today."

"On Saturday?"

"Yeah, because I'm flying down to Florida with you, and the presentation is on the twenty-seventh."

"Okay." She started out of the room then stopped and turned. "You want to come, Sarah?"

Sarah pressed her lips tightly together and shook her head.

Robin hated shopping. She hated it with a passion. Her wardrobe had all the basics; jeans, sweatshirts, T-shirts. She could purchase them without much thought, and best of all, quickly. Christmas shopping got tackled with the same simplicity -- something silky or lacy for Maxine, something simple or cute for Sarah.

Some wicked part of her mind taunted her with the thought that she needed to update her wardrobe for church, church functions and such, but she tried to drown it out and focus instead on the task at hand. As much as she hated shopping, she found herself in a dress shop in the mall a week before Christmas. Oh, that's right. In a dress shop in the mall a week before Christmas Day buying a dress so she could attend a Christmas party and have everyone there wondering where they've seen her before, then realizing that they knew her as that waitress from Benedicts' all "My Fair Ladied" up.

She audibly groaned when she realized that she hadn't even thought about buying Tony a Christmas present.

Great. Now she not only had to buy a dress, she had to buy a present for a man. What did one buy for a man? Especially a man who seemed to own the whole world?

"May I help you?"

She turned around and saw a salesclerk with brown hair and a Santa cap perkily perched on the top of her head. "Frankly, I hope you can, or I'm in big trouble."

"Well, let's see what we can do. What are you looking for?"

"A dress for a Christmas party."

"No problem." She managed to make the word 'no' into a six-syllable word. "Is it a formal party?"

Robin huffed out a breath. "I'm not positive, so my sister suggested I get a dress that could go either way."

The clerk looked her up and down. "Hmm. Let me think." Suddenly, her face lit up. "I've got it. Right this way. I think I have just the thing."

Robin had to dip into the savings account. Her rational mind wanted to feel guilty but her heart wouldn't let her. She figured once in her lifetime she could allow herself the luxury of spending a little too much money on a dress. And shoes. Robin flinched inwardly at the cost of the shoes. However, she felt certain that Maxine didn't have a silver pair she could borrow.

Her first Saturday off in ten years and she had to spend it at the stupid mall among throngs of holiday shoppers. She glanced at her watch, calculating that about five hours remained before she had to be ready for the party. Maybe she had enough time to figure out what to buy Tony for

Christmas. At least she could have this trip serve a dual purpose.

Before she'd even completed the thought, she saw it sitting in the window of a gift shop. Robin stopped in her tracks quickly enough that the person behind her nearly bumped into her. A panther carved out of some sort of black stone stared at her through the shop glass. Despite the solid stone, the way the muscles bunched, the head tilted down at a slight angle, it gave the impression of movement, as if it had just spotted its prey and moved closer for the kill.

Honestly, a more perfect gift didn't exist.

She dashed into the store, terrified that someone would buy it before she could get to it. People packed the store, and it took her a good ten minutes to find a clerk to take it off the display and package it for her.

As she left the store, she found herself cringing for the tenth time in the last five minutes. At least she no longer felt guilty about what she'd spent on the shoes. Robin quieted the numbers screaming in her mind. She forced herself not to care. She'd spent more money this afternoon on things other than necessities than she had spent in ten years, but it didn't matter. In her heart, she knew that Tony was worth it.

Robin stopped dead in her tracks in the middle of the crowded mall for the second time that day. When the realization came to her, came fully into focus in her conscious mind, it paralyzed her in the eye of a storm of conflicting thoughts and emotions such as she had never felt.

She loved Tony.

It felt right to think it, and terrifying. She felt like

maybe she'd always loved him. Wow. What did that mean in the whole scheme of things?

God had worked so hard on her heart that she had focused only on that and those feelings for months. She spent almost her entire relationship with Tony running from the conviction of God that she had not even noticed how her heart had also turned toward Tony.

As tears fell from her eyes, she silently thanked God for the revelation. Now what? Did she rush to Tony's side and confess all of these feelings? What if he didn't feel the same way? Wait! Of course he felt the same way.

Think of the way he treats you, she thought. Think of the way that he talks to you, and smiles at you, and touches you.

Except that if he really did love her the way she loved him, why wouldn't he have told her by now? His confidence overwhelmed her sometimes.

As holiday shoppers thronged around her and brushed by her, she analyzed it. He must have spent this whole time waiting for her to fall in love with God before he would allow himself to confess his love for her. She knew that they could not have a future if she never came to know Christ. In the week that followed, he had allowed her enough space to really soak in her newfound salvation and eternal security. He had spent their time together praying with her and teaching her and loving her the way that he always had.

She could not believe it, but could no longer deny it. She really loved him.

Her knees suddenly felt weak, and she looked around, spotting an unoccupied bench right beside her. She collapsed onto it before she draped the garment bag along the back of the bench and set the other bags at her feet. She'd just rest there for a minute. She needed to just rest.

What should she do now? Wait for him? Throw herself at him and confess her undying love? Even the thought of that made her giggle. She put her hands to her face and felt the silly grin and shook her head at herself. Giddy. Giddy in love. She wondered what would happen if she arrived at his office unannounced and suggested that he take her out to lunch. No, that plan wouldn't work. He had the big company Christmas party tonight and he likely found himself embroiled with all sorts of details about that. Managers and directors from all around the company had flown in and would spend the morning checking in to the hotel. She'd see him in a few hours. Maybe...

Just as she imagined how she would confess her love for Tony, someone sat next to her.

"Hiya, Robin."

She turned her head and managed a smile, though she sighed inwardly. "Hi, Sandy. Doing some Christmas shopping?"

She hadn't seen him since the week after the bar closed down at Hank's. She always found it odd seeing a bar patron in full light. The shadows in the dim bar always hid the flaws, and in Sandy's face, she could see the damage of years of alcoholism. The vessels on his face had broken, leaving little red marks. The skin around his eyes looked puffy and red and the whites of his eyes weren't quite white. She also noticed how much his hands shook.

"Actually, I was following you."

A touch of cautious fear twisted her stomach, but she kept her eyes steady and on his. She could handle Sandy. "Oh yeah? Why's that?"

He looked around him, his head moving in jerky movements. "Why don't we go somewhere more private?"

"No. I don't think so."

He leaned closer to her, and she had to hold her breath to keep from gagging on the stench of old beer that permeated the air around him. "You don't want to mess with me, little girl."

She rolled her eyes and chuckled while she adjusted her bags and stood. "What are you going to do to me, Sandy? Huh? Do us both a favor. Go home and sleep it off."

He stood with her, and for the first time, she realized how big he of a build he had. He stood a good head taller than her, but he also had a huge, bulky frame. He leaned down until his nose practically touched hers. "It's not what I can do to you, Robin, it's what my friends can do to your little sister. They're watching her right now, while she's at her parents' in Framingham. I just found out she's at the kitchen table, the one with the blue tablecloth, decorating Christmas cookies."

The finger of fear turned into a giant fist, tightening up and trembling in her gut. She believed him, and it terrified her. "Okay. Let's go somewhere more private."

He made a sweeping gesture with his arm, and she went ahead of him on stiff legs, through the mall, to the parking lot. Not knowing what else to do, she headed for her car. The whole time, he walked right behind her, half a step away, and her mind whirled while she tried to figure out what he wanted.

She stopped at her car and turned around, waiting for him to give her further direction. He did nothing but stuff his hands in the pockets of his worn coat and shiver against the bite in the air. Robin didn't even feel the cold.

"Do you know who I am?" he finally asked her.

She lifted her chin. "Should I?"

His eyes hardened. "I don't know why I thought that drunk slut would have told you anything about me." He huffed out a breath and rolled his eyes toward the gray sky. "I wouldn't have been caught if it hadn't been for her, anyway. I wouldn't have had to go to the pen for fifteen years if she hadn't screwed up the deal so bad. Still, not to tell a girl about her daddy, now that's just wrong."

Robin gasped and took a step backward. She opened her mouth, but no words came out. Then those watery eyes looked back at her. Eyes the same color as hers had years of alcohol abuse not dulled them. He smiled, his teeth yellow against his pale skin. "Ah, you're quick. Just like your daddy. I had to be quick. It's what's kept me from being caught this whole time."

Somehow she knew the answer, but she asked the question anyway. "Caught for what?" she whispered.

He went on as if he hadn't heard her. "See, I called her when I got out, thinking we could start all over. Man, she was a looker. But what a nagging—" He paused and shook his head. "I'd just scored big time, and we were going to hit it big. But she had that boyfriend she wanted to pull in on the deal. I didn't even know about him until we got back to the apartment. You can't even begin to imagine how angry that made me."

The air burned in her lungs. Suddenly, she could feel the cold and started shivering. She took another step away from him. "You killed them?"

He stepped forward. "He's the one who had the gun. He pulled it on me. I knew how to move back then and got it from him. The first shot was an accident. I swear it was.

Then I had to kill her, too, though. She knew who I was and I wasn't going back inside. No way was I going back."

He let out a shuddering breath. "All that's water under the bridge. All in the past," he said in a calmer voice. "I wanted to talk to you about the present."

She dropped the packages on the ground, wondering if she could take him. Fear kept her frozen, and she knew she couldn't. She also knew she couldn't risk Sarah. "What about it?"

"See, here's the deal." He suddenly showed signs of nervousness, and that terrified her even more. "I really worked on going straight, you know? I wasn't ever even going to tell you who I was. I figured, you'd work the bar and I'd get to know you, and in the meantime, I was doing whatever I could to keep it going, to have a roof over my head and still be able to pay my tab."

He calmed, grinned again. "The problem is, the straight and narrow ain't never worked for me. I slipped here and there, nothing major, but a deal's a deal, you know?" He fished a pack of cigarettes out of his pocket, and his hands shook badly enough that she wanted to take it away from him and get the cigarette out for him. "Then the bar closed down and I had all this free time. So, a few months ago, I got into something big. Only, I didn't know who I was dealing with, and they don't have a sense of humor about the money I skimmed off the top. I never touched the merchandise, never have. You gotta be stupid to touch the merchandise. I've always skimmed, though. Everybody does. You know, to cover expenses and what not."

He paused long enough to light the cigarette, then leaned against her car and hooked his thumb in the pocket of his dirty jeans as casually as if he discussed last night's football game. "Now I'm finding myself in a bit of a jamb. I have to come up with the money, see, all of it."

She rubbed at a throb that had suddenly appeared above her eye. "I don't have any money, Sandy."

He made a sound in the back of his throat like a strangled cough. "My name's Craig. Craig Bartlett."

She spoke with extreme patience, as one would to a child. "Okay, Craig. I don't have any money."

He laughed then bent over and coughed until his face turned beet red. He finally recovered and straightened. "I know you don't. I also know that your boyfriend does."

Ice clawed through her stomach and began working through her veins. "What are you talking about?"

"Oh, come on. You can't lie to your old man. I know. I been watching." He straightened and flicked the cigarette away. "Here's how it's going to work. Either ask him for the money or pilfer something we can hock. I don't care which. You do that, and you do it before Thursday. I have to pay these folks Friday morning. Got that? You got until Thursday."

"No way." She felt mad now, and the heat of anger started to thaw the ice.

He grabbed her by her shirt front and dragged her toward him. "Ten thousand. I need ten large by Thursday, or I hurt your sisters. I don't care which one, either. Neither of them's mine." He pushed her away and she staggered into her car. "Thursday," he repeated, then stalked away, leaving her standing there in the cold.

CHAPTER FIFTEEN

The dress had the faintest of silver snowflakes sewn into the ice blue satiny material. It had long tight sleeves hemmed at the wrist with silver thread and buttoned down the front with silver buttons in different snowflake shapes from the scooped neck down to where the dress stopped just below her knees. When she'd put it on in the store, she'd felt elegant and beautiful. Tonight she felt cheap and gaudy.

Robin managed to get her hair piled on top of her head and styled into a mass of curls secured by a silver clip on loan from Maxine. However, when she tried to apply her makeup, tremors kept going through her hands and she had to wipe it off and start over again twice.

She added lipstick and stood back from the mirror. No one looking at her would know that it had taken a full half an hour to apply the makeup, and only the facade mattered, anyway. She took a deep breath and slowly released it before she reached for the necklace, another loan from Maxine. The latch wouldn't catch, so she took another breath to try and steel her nerves, then tried again. Still nothing.

It all started to overwhelm her, and suddenly her world began to gray and her heart started racing. Then she heard the knock on the door and let out a strangled cry.

Steeling herself, she met her own eyes in the mirror and tried to give herself a little boost. Tonight was a big deal for Tony, and she could pretend she felt perfectly fine and dandy until tomorrow.

Secure in her ability to control her emotions, but not sure how much time had passed since the knock, she quickly moved through the apartment and threw open the door. There stood Tony, clad in his tuxedo, looking gorgeous and strong. Her eyes met his, and some calm returned. *Just remember the facade*, she told herself. This night belonged to Tony.

"Wow," he said. "You look absolutely beautiful. More than beautiful. Amazing."

She smiled and fought back the sting of tears. "Thank you. I actually went shopping this morning."

"You have both beautiful eyes and a good eye, *cara*," he said with a smile. "Problem?" he asked, gesturing at the necklace that she still had clutched in her hand.

"Yeah. The latch isn't working, or my hands aren't. One of the two."

He picked the necklace up and made a show of inspecting the latch he'd personally had Maxine rig while her spicy perfume wafted up and assaulted every sense he had. His hands shook and he thought about them all alone in the apartment. Then he thought about the hundreds of people waiting for him at the hotel, so he turned her toward the mirror by the door.

While she felt the cool metal go around her neck, she kept her eyes downcast, trying to find a way to get through the night.

"There," he said, "all fixed."

"Thanks, I don't know what was wrong with the stupid—" Her hand touched the choker as her eyes flew up to the mirror. She stared at her reflection with wide eyes before she slowly raised them to his. "Tony, I... you... I...."

Tony kissed the side of Robin's neck just below her ear and smiled. "It's perfect." He murmured. "You're perfect."

He turned her gently, but firmly, and he deliberately took her mouth with his. The slow languid kiss made her sigh. The sound vibrated through him. She stepped closer and wound her arms around his neck. A spark of desire ignited and spread through her middle. He abruptly broke contact and took a slight step back.

Robin closed her eyes and rested her forehead on his shoulder. "You need to quit giving me gifts like this."

He grinned and trailed a finger down her sleeve, over the pulse in her wrist and back up again. "Why?"

"Because I don't want you to think that I expect it." She raised her head and gripped the lapels of his coat and looked at him with eyes so intense they glittered. "That's not why I'm with you. I don't care about the jewelry or the money."

His eyes sobered as he tilted his head and looked at her. "I know that, Robin."

She jerked away and reached her hands behind her neck, fumbling with the clasp. "People will see me and they're going to think—"

"Stop!" He grabbed her wrists and jerked them down. "What does it matter? Huh?" He rolled his eyes over her head and muttered under his breath. "*Si un piccolo testardo.*"

She'd started working on learning Italian, and her eyes widened while she fought to keep up with the words as he rattled them out. "Did you just call me a little pig?"

"Pig headed. I called you pig headed, because I've already made it clear that I don't care what others think."

"People will—"

"So what?" He realized the level to which they'd raised their voices and took a deep steadying breath. "We know. You and I know. Us. God knows. That's all that counts."

She breathed in and out, concentrating on fighting off the panic. "Okay." Another breath, in and out. She nodded. "Okay, I'm sorry. I guess I'm just nervous."

He smiled and kissed her one more time. "Everyone will love you." *Like I do*, he silently added. "I have no doubt."

Wanting to lighten the mood, she pushed away and grabbed her clutch bag. She pulled out her lipstick tube, intending to repair the damage of his kisses. "Except those who call me a pig."

He laughed and kissed the top of her head before gathering her coat from the back of the couch. "The exact translation was you're a little pig headed fool."

She snorted while she laughed and tried to hold her arms steady through the gale while he helped her put on her coat.

Barry watched them walk into the ballroom arm in

arm—the tall, dark Italian with the cool, slim blonde. Even he, skeptic of their relationship, could see how well they looked together and could see the way his friend practically hovered over her as they worked the room. His touches were casual but constant—a brush on her cheek here, a hand at the small of her back there, and Barry relaxed further when he saw how Robin responded, how she leaned into Tony or smiled a smile just for him. They communicated through touches as though they'd married for years, and for the first time, Barry began to rethink his earlier opinion.

Deciding that he'd observed from a distance long enough, he headed in their direction. The party consisted of all of the people who ran the individual companies of Viscolli Enterprises across the country, and their spouses or companions, not only because Tony put on a good party, but because there existed an implied mandatory nature of the event. Part of the annual budget for the party consisted of the airplane tickets and lodgings. They all knew Barry and several accosted him with different legal questions. At one point, he lost sight of the couple while he talked to a manager and his deejay wife from a west coast radio station Tony owned. Finally, though, he managed to make it to them.

They stood in a corner alone for the first time since arriving. Barry watched Tony turn his head and whisper into her ear before he looked up and saw Barry's approach. He felt that conversation they'd had about Robin the right conversation at the time. Still felt that way. However, he couldn't help feeling relieved when Tony's eyes warmed.

"Barry. I was wondering where you were." He looked over Barry's shoulder. "Where's Jacqueline?"

Barry looked at his watch. "She should be landing in Zurich within the hour."

Tony raised an eyebrow. "Christmas in the Alps this year?"

"Apparently." His lips formed a hard line. "My flight will leave Tuesday morning."

Tony slipped an arm around Robin's back. "Robin, you haven't officially met Barry Anderson, Viscolli's lawyer and, I'm proud to say, a personal friend. My best friend, in fact."

Robin remembered the last time she'd seen the giant now standing in front of her. She'd seen him in Hank's kitchen and he had defended Tony when she claimed that Tony insinuated that she could be bought. Her cheeks flushed a little at the memory. "You're the Shirley Temple," she said with a big smile, hoping to cover some of her uneasiness.

Barry cleared his throat and squeezed her outstretched hand. "How can you even remember that?"

"It was just surprising that a guy who looked like a linebacker would order that drink. I guess it stood out." She noticed the same drink in his hand and laughed. "Anyway, it's nice to meet you. Tony speaks of you often."

Robin imagined he could look really mean if he gave it half an effort, but after so many years with Hank, his size did nothing to intimidate her. She could see the kindness in his eyes, and immediately liked him, though she couldn't help shifting under his appraisal.

"I wouldn't have recognized you if I hadn't known who you were," he said, finally releasing her hand.

She gestured at the dress. "Well, it's a far cry from a tuxedo shirt and slacks." She leaned closer to him. "But I'll confess that I'd be more comfortable." She shifted her feet in the silver heels. "Especially in those ugly shoes. I miss my ugly shoes."

The longer Barry spoke with her, the further Tony relaxed. He checked his watch. "It's about time for me to give my yearly pep talk." He glanced around the room until he made eye contact with someone and nodded. "Why don't you two go sit at the table and we'll get the party started."

Robin hooked her arm through Barry's. "How uncouth would it be for me to kick my shoes off at the table?"

"Your feet don't smell do they?"

"Of course not. My nose smells. My feet walk."

Barry patted her hand while Tony followed behind them. "In that case, anyone who wants to say anything will have to come through me."

She laughed and glanced back over her shoulder at Tony. He looked so relaxed, so at ease, and she vowed to keep the simulated smile solidly on her face, no matter what.

Silence cloaked the interior of the limo while Robin toyed with the choker around her neck and stared out of the window. Tony stayed quiet himself, choosing to just watch her while the car cut through the quiet streets. He'd known something had weighed heavily on her earlier in the day and had assumed it nerves from the party the main culprit, but as the evening wore on, he watched her become more and more tense. He watched all night and whenever he hadn't seen her actively engaged in speaking with someone or laughing just a second too long at something someone said, her face sobered up and a few times she appeared on the verge of tears.

Neither spoke when the car pulled up to her apartment building or when the driver let them out. They held hands as they climbed the stairs to her floor and walked, slowly, down the hallway to her door. She slipped one shoe off in the hall outside of her apartment, leaning into Tony when she wobbled on one foot and peeled the other shoe off, but still never spoke a word. Tony decided he would break the silence. He took her key from her and unlocked the door but didn't open it.

"May I make an observation?" He asked, leaning against the wall by the door.

Robin raised her eyes from the ugly green and orange design in the carpet to look at him. "Sure."

"You wouldn't be able to play poker. Every single thought you have is written all over your face the very instant you think it."

Her head started spinning. She smiled a smile that hurt her face and stepped forward to run a finger over his bow-tie. "Then you know what I'm thinking right now," she said.

He covered her hand with one of his and waited until she raised her eyes to look at him. "Yes, I can tell what you're thinking now. I know you're trying to distract me because something is seriously bothering you. And I know it's something important."

She raised an eyebrow. "Can you also tell that I don't want to talk about it?"

He closed his eyes and sighed before looking at her again. "I wish you would."

He didn't resist when she pulled her hands out from

under his. Framing his face with her hands, she kissed his unyielding lips. "I don't know how." She tried to kiss him again but he didn't give in. Finally, she stepped back. "I really wanted to wait until tomorrow. This was your big night." She opened the door and stepped into her apartment. "Can you please come in?"

After a moment of hesitation, he stepped inside. In the late hour, the apartment lay dark and silent. Robin knew her sisters lay sleeping in their shared room, so she kept her voice low as she and Tony sat on her love seat, their bodies turned toward each other. "Would you mind terribly if I said I didn't really want to go to Florida?"

Tony reached out and took her hand. "Your hands are like ice," he observed, sandwiching her hand between both of his, sharing his warmth. "Depends. Would you go if I said I had to go, regardless?"

She stared at his face, his handsome face, his beautiful face and thanked God for giving him to her. "I want to spend Christmas with you, but Sarah can't come."

She felt the sting of tears in her eyes. "I really need to go. I've been neglecting it, but it can wait until after the holiday, *cara mia*. I will spend Christmas wherever you are." Relief immediately flooded her heart. He frowned at her. "What is wrong, *cara*?"

Robin felt the tears flood her eyes and spill down her cheeks. She ripped her hand from his and scrubbed at both cheeks. "I'm afraid to talk about it." She sobbed.

He pulled her close. "I can't fix it if I don't know what it is."

Overwhelmed, Robin couldn't hear the love in his voice, didn't feel the security of his arms. She just knew he would regret starting this relationship with the daughter of a murdering extortionist. "You're going to hate me."

She felt his deep intake of breath and the slow release. "I can assure you that I will not hate you." He kissed the top of her head and pushed her back so that he could frame her face with his hands. She looked up at him, at his face, and could see the sincerity in his eyes. "Listen to me. Whatever it is, between me and God, we can fix it. You just have to talk to us. Trust Him and trust me. But don't despair."

Despair. How could he have worded it more perfectly? She pulled away from him and launched to her feet. Needing to move, she went into the little kitchenette and poured them each a glass of water. Glad to have something to do with her hands, she returned to the living room and set the glasses on the coffee table, but did not sit down.

She briefly left the living room and went to her room. The bags she'd brought in the previous afternoon still sat on her bed, a carnage of hangers and boxes and tissue paper left over from her getting ready for the party. She searched through them until she found the one from the gift shop. She wished, now, that she'd taken the clerk up on her offer to wrap the gift, but she'd wanted to do it herself. Now its package would have to serve as the bag.

When she returned to the living room, she found Tony standing by the couch. She set the bag on the coffee table and sat down.

"This is your Christmas present," she said, pushing it toward him. "I'd like for you to open it now."

She could sense his irritation and impatience. "Christmas is a week away."

She blinked and continued as if he hadn't spoken. "I was almost desperate. I mean, what do you get someone who has everything? I knew it had to be something special. Then I saw it."

He stared at the bag. She waited ten seconds, then thirty, then sixty, wanting to rip it open for him. Finally, with a lukewarm smile and leisurely movements, he sat back down on the couch and reached for and then opened the bag.

Tony lifted the panther out and tossed the bag somewhere behind him before gently setting the sleek black cat on the table in front of him. He ran his hand along its back, tracing the line of muscles that looked ready to spring. When he finally looked back up at Robin, his eyes nearly matched the color of the stone. She almost gasped.

He didn't speak, just looked back down at the statue. Then he took a sip of his water. She cleared her throat. "It reminded me of you." His eyes flew back up to hers and she hurried on to get out what she had to say. "Its strength is there, shimmering just under the surface, but it's contained—controlled. You're like that, you know? I can't really explain it. And those eyes—so intense they're nearly scary."

His hand ran along the back of the statue again. "Thank you, Robin."

On the bar between the living room and kitchen, she spotted one of her tins of peppermints. She moved over to the bar and opened it. "My father was put in prison for cocaine trafficking when my mother was pregnant with me."

She pulled a peppermint out of the tin and toyed with it before putting it in her mouth and sucking on it. "She was a horrible woman. I can't even begin to describe it to you."

When Robin looked up she found him watching her

intently, staring. "Well, maybe I don't need to describe it to you. Maybe you already know." Nothing on his face changed, so she continued. "She was abusive, loud, harsh, neglectful. She used men and drugs. Men provided places to live, and income for drugs. She provided whatever it was they wanted in their sick minds. My earliest memories were hiding from her or the boyfriend of the week—and holding Maxi, then holding Maxi and Sarah. I remember cowering in this dark closet cradling Maxi to me, praying she wouldn't wake up and give away our hiding spot. I couldn't have been much more than three or four, and the noises coming from the outside of the closet—"

She cleared her throat and looked back down at the little metal tin. "When I was fifteen, my mother and her boyfriend were murdered." Finding some reserves of courage, she looked at him again. "He was a really bad guy. He…" She cleared her throat again and rolled the mint on her tongue. "He would come to my bed at night after mom passed out and…." her breath hitched and she stopped speaking.

Tony's eyes came to life as if someone had flipped a switch. Heat burned behind them and his jaw set like iron. In that heartbeat, she knew that if her father hadn't already killed the man, Tony would have hunted him down. She didn't know how she felt about that so she didn't finish the sentence.

"We were all back in that closet. It wasn't the same closet, but they were all the same, really. Dark, smelly, sometimes there were things in there scurrying through the walls or on shelves above our heads. I'd taught Maxine and Sarah how to hide, how to get way back in the back against the back wall. Out of sight, out of mind, you know? He was trying to get me. My mother had left hours before, and by then he was good and drunk and he decided he wanted me to scratch an itch."

Robin spoke as if the events she related had happened to someone else. Occasionally, she sucked on her peppermint, letting the cooling mint soothe her taste buds as if she wanted to cleanse her mouth of a bad taste left behind by speaking about these memories. "I managed to kick him in the groin, and ran to the closet. I hadn't been in there long when we heard our mother come back. She had another man with her. There was an argument, and then gunshots. Then it was so quiet. I felt like I couldn't breathe, and Maxi and Sarah were so strong and so good." Her voice hitched and for a moment, just a moment, she was fifteen again and trying her best to protect those two precious children. "When the police found us and pulled us out of the closet, we learned that our mother and her boyfriend had both been shot dead.

"Sarah got adopted. Maxi and I made it in the system. The first place was bad." Another dark memory surged to the surface but she beat it back—a memory for another time. "Maxi and I were separated and I was put into a girls' home. I ran away when I turned eighteen. Hank gave me a job and he helped me get Maxine out, helped me keep her safe. Eventually, I got visitation with Sarah and for one hour a month, my family was together and I never really gave my mother much of another thought. I knew I would do anything in my power not to be like her, not to be used like her. All these years, and I never even cared who killed her." She sat again folded her hands in her lap. "Really, it was kind of a relief."

Tony reached forward and covered both of her hands

with one of his. "Why haven't you ever told me this before?"

With a weak shrug, she said, "It's one thing to pull yourself off the streets and become what you've become. It's another to be a victim your entire life. That's why I did what I did, Tony. I got Maxi and I supported her, then I put her through college. I worked my tail off so she wouldn't ever have to be like our mother. She can count on me and she will never need a man to survive."

Robin watched Tony's eyebrows rise as he took in this concept, this motivation. "Then I talked Sarah's parents into letting me help her. It was hard, and exhausting, and there were times I just wanted to cry and cry because I was so tired and tuition and books cost so much and they needed to be secure."

"But you didn't cry."

She shook her head. "I couldn't. That would have been the ultimate feminine weakness. Cry when the chips get you down." She turned her hand and linked his fingers with hers.

He raised their joined hands and placed a kiss on the back of hers. Her heart did a flip-flop at the gesture. "What else? There's more."

"This afternoon at the mall, an old bar regular from Hank's approached me. He's a little annoying, but I never gave him too much of a thought. He paid his tab every night, and other than trying to hold my attention too much, he was nothing to me. A nobody." She pulled her hand from his and stood again, then started pacing. "He told me—" Her breath hitched and she spun around and looked at him. "He told me I had to go with him. He told me he had friends, that they were watching Sarah. He even described the room she was in."

Tony straightened. "Go on," he said in a tight voice.

"He took me out into the parking lot. He... he..."

In one move, Tony stood in front of her, gripping her shoulders. "What? What did he do?"

Robin looked at the intensity on his face, horrified at what would come next. "He told me he was my father. He told me that he killed my mother. He told me he would kill one of my sisters if I didn't give him ten thousand dollars by Thursday." She spoke as quickly as she could, never realizing that tears streamed down her face.

He gripped her shoulders hard enough to bruise but she didn't realize that either. "What did you say to him?"

"I... I... I t-t-told him I d-d-didn't have any money," she managed to get out.

"And?" He gave her a small shake. "And what, Robin?"

"He... he... he... Oh dear God in heaven, you're going to hate me. I'm sorry. I'm so sorry."

"Robin, what else?"

She thought she might throw up. "He said you had money." She covered her face with her hands and sobbed. "I don't know what to do, Tony." He pulled her to him and wrapped his arms around her. "I don't know what to do."

"Shhh. Shush, now, *cara*. Don't worry." His voice sounded steely, hard. "I know exactly what to do."

CHAPTER SIXTEEN

Tony sat in his apartment on his couch. He kept the shades drawn and all of the lights in the room extinguished, with the exception of the dimmed track lighting above the couch. Late morning had come and gone, but Tony did not feel fatigue yet. He sat back against the leather, staring at the panther on the table in front of him.

Tony ceased the continual praying in his spirit for the first time since the day he gave his life over to Christ. He shut it down as the all too human emotion of the need for retribution flooded through his heart. He felt his mouth thin as he refused to seek counsel from the Holy Spirit, knowing without asking that he would not receive approval for his decided course of action.

He had finally managed to soothe Robin out of the panic that caused her hysteria and calmed her down, assuring her that he did not hate her. After he persuaded her to go to bed, he let himself out of the apartment.

Tony made eye contact with the statue. Yes, he could see the similarities there, just as she'd seen. Only they shared more that she hadn't touched on, perhaps because she didn't know. He also enjoyed the natural territorial instinct of the cat. He also commanded the ruthlessness that only true predators possessed, either when they hungered or when an intruder breached their territory.

She had thought that he would hate her because someone wanted to use her to get to him. He knew it had taken a lot for her to tell him. Robin wasn't the type of woman who would easily turn to someone, anyone, for help.

She had looked to him. That meant more to him coming from her than a declaration of love would ever mean. He would take care of it. He would take care of her. Just as the panther in front of him would handle any foe that foolishly encroached upon his territory. He leaned his head back and stared at the ceiling making plans, deciding on a course of action.

When he knew what he had to do and how to do it, he checked his watch and called Robin. She answered with a sleepy voice on the fourth ring, and he felt a pang of regret for waking her. "Hello, *cara*. I'm sorry I woke you."

"No. Don't be sorry." He could hear the shifting of the bedcovers and could picture her sitting up in the bed.

"I only wanted to ask if you could meet me at church. If not, I could send a car for you, but I have an errand to run and won't be able to get to your side of town."

"No, that's okay. I'll drive."

He smiled so that she would hear it in his voice. "Wonderful. I can't wait to see you."

They said their good-byes and he hung up the phone. With a last glance at the predatory cat on his coffee table, he stood and moved to his dressing room to prepare for the day.

Tony headed deep into his old neighborhood, driving slowly. As he passed the church, he noticed that the parking lot had a scattering of cars in it already. He knew he had another thirty minutes before time to greet students in his classroom. At the moment, he couldn't even remember what he planned to teach that morning. Instead, he focused on the task at hand. He turned at the corner, drove another quarter of a mile, then turned down another street, relishing in the dark thoughts that surfaced as the memories assaulted him. He needed dark thoughts right now.

He pulled up to the curb in front of a dilapidated building. As soon as he stepped out of the car, a group of teenagers surrounded it. Cars like that, shiny black sports cars that cost more than ninety percent of the country could afford just didn't park in front of this building.

He picked the one with the meanest eyes and stabbed his gloved finger at him. "You." He pulled a bill out of his pocket. "You see this?" he asked. The kid sneered and nodded at the hundred-dollar bill Tony held. "You get ten of these if this car is exactly the same when I come out."

"Why should I trust you?"

Tony shrugged. "The same reason I'm trusting you." He walked inside without a backward glance. He didn't even bother to lock the doors on the car.

The door opened at eight forty-five on a Sunday morning. Jake's Bar stayed open twenty-four hours a day, seven days a week, and Tony had a strong feeling that he would find the person he sought here.

He removed his dark shades just as he walked inside to start the process of letting his eyes adjust to the murky darkness within. It took real effort to keep his nose from curling at the stench of a bar where spilled beer rarely got mopped up and most of the patrons didn't care whether they'd showered that week or not. His eyes scanned the room, noting the possible conflicts and searching for the familiar face. He found him at the far end of the bar with an unlit cigarette dangling out of his mouth and greasy hair falling into his eyes.

The bartender paused and watched him walk the length of the room, measuring him up. Tony met his eyes and, finally, recognition dawned on Jake's face. Once recognition hit, he grinned, choosing, Tony guessed, to ignore the fact that the last time he'd seen Tony he'd told him he'd kill him if he ever saw him near his joint again. Money and influence coaxed a lot of people into bouts of amnesia.

"Well, well, well," Jake said, "Look who decided to grace my doorway, again. What can I get you, Tony?"

"Whatever he's drinking," he said, gesturing at his target. He reached the end of the bar and leaned his hand on the grimy surface, trapping the weasel in front of him in the corner. "Hi, Billy. Remember me?"

Nervous eyes darted up and back down again. "Yeah. Sure. Who doesn't? You're a neighborhood legend." Billy's eyes darted around, perhaps looking to see if Tony had brought along any muscle. "Whatcha doin' here?"

"Who says I can't just drop by and catch up with old friends?" He ignored the glass that Jake slid toward him and leaned closer. "I never forget anyone who ripped me off, Billy. I distinctly remember you ripping me off."

Billy's eyes skirted around, never resting on Tony. "What does it matter to you, anyway? You got out. You're living high and mighty now, right?"

He pulled out a fifty-dollar bill. "Seems like you ripped me off for ten times this amount, didn't you, Billy boy?"

"Oh man!" He grabbed Tony's drink and downed it in one swallow. Tony looked up and nodded for Jake to pour another one. "Whatcha want, man? Just get to it without the games."

Tony leaned closer. "I need info. I also need someone to spread some info around."

"I don't know nothing."

"You owe me. Don't forget that." He reached into the pocket of his overcoat and pulled out a wad of fifties. "And I pay. Twice this much if you do it right."

Billy stared at the money, his eyes bugging like a strangled mouse. "Okay." He nodded, reminding Tony of a chicken. "Okay. Whatcha need to know?"

"I need to know who Craig Bartlett owes."

"What makes you think I know?"

"Billy, you know everything. Your slimy little ears are pressed to the ground more than anyone else's." He raised an eyebrow. "Unless you've lost your touch."

Billy stared at the bills and licked his lips. "Okay. Okay. Word is he owes Junior Mills."

"Who's Junior Mills?"

"God man, you've been gone too long." He took the

fresh drink and swallowed it all. "Old man Jacob Mills bit the dust years ago. Apparently, some of the local bulls gave him a free stick therapy session and he saw the light long enough to recall the names of some southern gentlemen. After that, I hear his shoes got heavy and pulled him to the bottom of Boston harbor."

Tony felt a pang of the past. He had once worked for Jacob Mills, stole a few cars for him. Who could have foreseen that Jacob's untimely end would come at the hands of some South American drug lord?

Billy still squealed. "Junior took over, and he's meaner than his daddy could ever have hoped to be. Can't stand a cop. Just as soon plug one as pay him off. Word is Bartlett skimmed off the top of a deal and Junior blew him a kiss."

Tony shrugged. "Everybody skims. Cost of doing business."

Billy looked like he had no idea what to do with his hands. "I guess it depends on who ends up with the twenty and who ends up with the eighty."

"Eighty percent of the take? Jacob would have used the guy to fertilize his lawn."

"Yeah," Billy agreed sagely. "But Junior isn't as nice as his old man was."

Tony held up a finger signaling Jake to pour one more drink. Billy started feeling the confidence that only came with two straight shots spaced out over seconds. He sneered at Tony and nodded his head. "Looks like you have your ear in places, too."

"Nah. This is personal." He pushed the stack of money Billy's way and pulled an identical one out of his pocket. "You spread my message the way I tell you, and I'll see that you get this one, too."

The money in front of Billy disappeared faster than snow in Miami. "Hey, sure. Anything for you, old buddy."

"You tell anyone who will listen that Bartlett is talking big about skimming from Junior. You add that he said no one could have ever skimmed the old man. You got that?"

Billy snorted and laughed. "You want Bartlett killed or something?"

Tony stared at the little drunk. "Or something."

"Oh, Jeez." Billy breathed.

"Then you say how Bartlett knows that Junior has it out for him and he's thinking about going to the cops with it before the deadline." He looked up and nodded at Jake then leaned even closer to Billy. "You got it, Billy? Then you let Bartlett know he can find me at Hank's place, out by the college."

"Sure. When do I get the rest of my money?"

Tony straightened, pushed the fresh drink toward Billy, and tossed a bill for the tab toward Jake. "When I know the message has been sent."

Billy didn't drink the whole thing this time. He took a small sip and smiled up at Tony. "Hey man, sorry about the whole thing from all those years ago. I'm glad it's forgotten."

"The only way we're square, Billy, is if you do what I asked you. Otherwise, I may start holding you in the same high regard I have for my good friend Bartlett." He pushed away from the bar.

"Sure, Tony, sure. I'll spread the word."

"*Ciao.*" He slipped his glasses back on as he pushed his way outside.

His car had remained in its original position, and the kid with the mean eyes leaned against the hood. Two of his friends lay sprawled, unconscious, in uncomfortable looking positions on the street and sidewalk. He didn't see the other two. Tony looked the lad up and down, seeing a reflection of himself fifteen years earlier.

"Your friends look tired," Tony observed.

"They aren't my friends," the youth answered dryly.

Tony smiled, "What's your name?"

"Derrick. Derrick DiNunzio" He gestured at the unconscious pair. "I don't think these guys trusted you."

Tony looked around, up at the buildings, down the street. Something about this kid tugged at his heart. He tried to ignore it, but something deep inside wouldn't let him. "Do you have any friends around here, Derrick? Any family? Do you like living here?"

Derrick shrugged and stuffed his hands into the pockets of the old black leather jacket he wore. It had a hole in the right elbow. "Don't have a choice for now. But I ain't staying for long. I'm getting out." He looked at the car and back at Tony. "Just like you did. I'll go straight and narrow like you and make my break."

Tony liked the desire to go straight and narrow. He raised an eyebrow at the recognition. "How old are you?"

"Eighteen." Tony just stared. Derrick raised his chin defiantly. "Almost."

Tony pulled a business card out of his pocket. He scribbled a note on the back of it and set it atop the folded bills. "Come see me when it's a little more than almost. I may have something for you."

"You suddenly have a CIO position open up?"

Tony stopped short and barked a quick laugh.

"What would you want me doing for you, Mr. Tony Viscolli? Clean your toilets? Polish your silverware?"

Tony opened the car door and smiled. "Guess you'll just have to trust me."

He drove quickly, the desire to leave the stench of the past behind him helped him press the accelerator harder. He needed to get to church. He just wished he could shower beforehand.

Right before he turned the corner, he looked in his rearview mirror and saw Derrick still standing where he'd left him, the business card in one hand and the money in the other. The kid stared at the card. Tony grinned, turned the heater up higher, and flipped the radio on, finding a good, loud jazz station.

Tony sat in Barry's weight room while his friend huffed his way through his last set of bench pressing one-hundred-twenty-pound weights. He had canceled his Monday morning appointments and had come straight to Barry's house.

Barry had a weight room built into his house that rivaled any gymnasium around. Glass walls reflected state-of-the-art equipment. A large screen television hung on the wall in front of the treadmill, stationary bike, and rowing machine. At the moment, Mozart's Requiem pumped through the speakers, surrounding the room with the classical sounds.

Barry sat up and wiped his face with a towel. He looked at his friend closely. "What's wrong?"

Tony inspected his fingernails. "Why would you assume something is wrong?"

Barry laughed and tossed his towel around his neck. "You're wearing jeans and it's Monday. I'm trying to remember if I've ever personally seen you in jeans. Maybe, one time, when—no, wait, you wore Dockers."

Tony had a hard time seeing the humor. "What does that have to do with anything?"

"Nothing other than the fact that you always look like you're about to model for a cover shoot for GQ, no matter what, and you're sitting here on one of your busiest work days wearing blue jeans and you don't look like you've shaved. Consequently, I'm assuming that something is wrong."

Tony pushed himself off of the weight bench and paced the room. The problem with this room, he decided, was that he could not escape his reflection. Everywhere he looked, he could see himself. Of course, everywhere he saw himself, he saw a man filthy with sin.

He stopped in front of a wall and stared. His bloodshot eyes dimly glared back at him. The weight on his heart made it hard to stand up straight. He could not run from the conviction for another moment. "I've done something that cannot be undone."

Intrigued, Barry drained a bottle of water and tossed the empty plastic bottle into a trash can that stood next to the door to the restroom. "Nothing is undoable. Unless, of course, you murdered someone."

He said the last thing as a joke, but his friend's shoulders slumped forward slightly and he sighed heavily. Barry froze. No way. "Tony?"

Tony turned, moving like an old man. "I haven't

murdered anyone yet, but I certainly signed his death warrant."

Barry cocked his head, trying to find another angle to look at his friend. His best friend. "I think you need to be a little more specific."

With his hands covering his face, Tony leaned against the mirrored wall and slid down until he sat on his heels. He rubbed his eyes, tired from two nights of no sleep, and finally lowered his hands. Barry sat next to him, waiting. Tony took a deep breath, and plunged forward, telling Barry about Robin's story and his own trip to the old neighborhood.

Barry sat quietly long after Tony finished speaking. He didn't look at him. Instead, he looked forward, staring at Tony's reflection in the opposite wall. Finally, he said, "Why did you do that?"

Tony wanted to shrug. He wanted to get angry and storm away from the judgment that he so rightfully felt directed his way. He wanted to do a lot of things. Instead, he leaned his head back and closed his eyes. "Because I was angry."

Barry nodded. "There are a lot of things I need to say to you right now. I think you know most of them. I think you know that this relationship you had with Robin wasn't good for you in a lot of ways. I am very happy she's accepted Christ now and can start growing in the Lord, but until she did that, there wasn't anything good about being with her. I think that because you determined to be the one responsible for her eternal destiny, that you almost created an idol of your feelings for her. Because of that, it opened a place in your heart where the enemy could worm his way in and break you."

Tony felt every single word as if Barry stabbed his heart with an ice pick at every syllable. He spoke the truth, and Tony knew it. Barry continued. "You are a powerful force in God's kingdom, Tony. You have money, influence, prestige, and you pour it back to God without hesitation. You know as well as I know that you are a constant target, and for some reason when this woman came into your life, you seemed to forget that."

Tony rolled his head until he looked at Barry directly. Barry's mouth thinned in a disapproving line, then relaxed again. His next words surprised Tony. "The awesome thing about God is that He is a forgiving God. If you repent, your slate will once again be wiped clean."

Emotions clutched Tony's throat and he felt his eyes burn. He shoved the heels of his hands against his eyes. "That doesn't change this."

"No. It doesn't change this."

They sat in silence for a long time. Tony's emotions slowly overwhelmed him until he rocked forward and landed on his knees, then continued forward until he bowed in humbled posture before God. He didn't realize he'd begun praying out loud until he felt Barry next to him praying along with him. He prayed for forgiveness first and foremost. Then he prayed for help. He begged God to help him figure out what to do next, how to fix it, how to set it right.

After a long time, he simply fell silent in meditation and Barry left him alone so that he would have no distractions from hearing God's voice.

CHAPTER SEVENTEEN

Robin stood in her office and stared at a framed picture of her and her sisters. She didn't put it there, so one of them must have. A friend of Maxine's had snapped a picture of them at Maxi's college graduation party. Robin tilted her head and tried to look at it from maybe another angle, but it still looked the same. They looked like three perfectly normal women. They didn't look like the offspring of a murderer, a drug dealer, a prostitute. They just looked normal.

She turned back to face the room and saw Barry look at his watch. Tony sat in her chair behind her desk, where she had insisted that he sit, spinning his gold pen on her blotter. They had spent the last thirty minutes praying together—praying for help, wisdom, strength, courage. Since ending the prayer, though, no one had spoken. The silence in the room hovered heavy and thick, and she really couldn't stand it much longer.

"Tony said you're going to the Alps for Christmas?" she asked of Barry.

His head shot up and for a moment his eyes did not focus on her. When they did, he smiled slightly. "My wife enjoys travel. I guess the Alps are this year's hot spot for Christmas."

He said it with a twist to his lips. Years of public service had taught her well how to read people, and she thought better of pursuing the conversation. "Tony invited me and my sisters to the Keys with him this year, but we can't go."

"Yes you can," Tony said.

She looked at him and shook her head. "No. Remember? I told you that Sarah can't go."

He waved a hand. "She's going to come and then leave on Christmas Eve. It's already taken care of."

Robin ran her tongue over her upper lip. "That's an awful lot of flying for your pilot."

"He's a pilot. That's what he does. He's complained I haven't flown him as much as usual this year." His eyes warmed. "I've been sticking too close to Bean Town." Robin flushed knowing that he had adjusted his schedule so much for her. Tony laughed. "Besides, he was already flying back because his family is here, so she's just catching a ride with him. We'll stay until the day after Christmas like we planned."

Barry surged to his feet. "How can you two just chit chat idly by when…?"

A knock at the door interrupted him. At Robin's beckoning, the hostess popped her head in. "There's someone out here asking for you, Robin."

Robin put her hand to her stomach and took a deep breath. "I'll be right out."

Barry moved with purpose to the door, closing the distance in two strides. "Let's get this over with." He held the door for Robin, then followed her out. Tony stayed. He murmured once they entered the hallway leading to the dining area. "You just look at me if you need help," he said, pausing by the huge Christmas tree that stood in the corner next to a grand piano.

Robin pressed her lips into a thin line and nodded stiffly. The hostess had seated Sandy—Craig—where she'd asked her to, and she had a clear view of him. He hadn't seen her yet. She watched as he drained his glass of ice water and looked behind him, then fidgeted with the glass and looked behind him again, then looked at his watch.

"You'd better get over there," Barry said.

"I hope this works," she said, and started walking. Until the moment Sandy saw her, she thought she might run away, but the second his watery blue eyes met hers, she relaxed. She felt God place a mantle of peace over her shoulders as if it had been a physical thing.

She pulled out the chair across from him and sat down. "Hi, Craig."

His knee started jerking up and down and his thumb tapped a rhythm on the tablecloth. "Remember when we used to play games? Like I give you the name of a drink and you give me what it's made out of?"

"Sure. Of course I remember."

"Good. I got one for you."

Confused, Robin tipped her head. "Okay."

"Dead Man Walking."

She gave a short shake of her head. "I'm afraid I don't know that one. I guess you finally stumped me."

"Dead Man Walking. That's me. The heat on the street is turned up. I need my ten large now."

Standing, Robin nodded. "Come on back to my office, Craig."

All of his nervous, jerky movement stopped. Suddenly. He sat completely still for a moment, then he smiled, showing a mouth full of yellow teeth. "You got it? That's my girl!"

As she led the way to her office, he babbled on behind her. "I wasn't sure you'd go for it, you know? You weren't exactly receptive to my offer the other day. All along, though, I knew you'd come through for your old man. I knew it!"

She opened the door and stepped aside, allowing him to precede her into the room. He stopped short the second that he saw Tony sitting at Robin's desk. "Hey now," he said. He turned to leave the room but found his exit blocked by Barry. "What's this?"

Tony stood and gestured to the chairs in front of the desk. "Mr. Bartlett, please sit down."

He balled his fists and his face turned bright red. "I ain't…"

Tony reached into the open desk drawer and pulled out a stack of money. Ten thousand dollars in one hundred dollar bills. Craig stopped, licked his lips, and sat in a chair.

Tony leaned back and the chair squeaked with his weight. "You obviously know that I've been seeing your daughter."

"Yeah. I been keepin' an eye on her. I know what's what."

"If you know what's what, then you know who I am."

"Of course." Craig licked his lips and looked at the money again.

Tony reached out and laid his fingers on his pen, but kept it still. "I'm going to give you this money, but I'm going to do it on two conditions."

Craig's leg started moving up and down again in a fast, jerky rhythm. "Yeah. Sure. Whatever you want."

"Number one, you never, ever, ask for money again. If you ever do, then Robin or I will go to the police and file a complaint about extortion."

Robin watched as his leg paused momentarily before beating an even faster beat. "Yeah. Yeah. Okay. Thanks." He stood and reached for the money. Tony held up his hand and Craig slowly sat back down. "Right. Two conditions. Okay. What's numero two?"

Tony sat forward and laced his fingers together. "That you allow me to pray for you right now."

Craig's entire body went still before he threw his head back and laughed. "What? What did you say?"

"I said that you can have this money if you never ask for money again and if you allow me to pray for you right here and right now."

Still laughing, Craig nodded. "Fine. Yeah, sure. Whatever. Go for it."

Robin stood next to Barry and watched as Tony got up from behind the desk and walked over to Craig. He stood next to him and placed a hand on his shoulder, then bowed his head. "Father God," he said, then began a beautiful prayer of petition to God for Craig's life, for sobriety, for the removal of the scales from his eyes, for discernment, for salvation, for grace—he prayed for twenty minutes and Robin watched in awe and wonder as Craig's fidgety body stilled. Several moments passed while he just sat there staring at the money, but eventually he closed his eyes and bowed his head.

When Tony finished, Craig surged to his feet. "You's guys, you're all crazy." He snatched up the money and shoved it in his pockets. He laughed a mean laugh. "It was a pleasure doing business with ya."

As he left the office, he stopped in front of Robin. She didn't know what she expected to hear from her father's mouth, but what he said had her gasping in horror. "Tell that pretty little sister of yours I said hi."

He slammed the door behind him as he left. The silence in the office felt heavy, weird, then Barry let out a loud breath. "Well, next time he comes around let me know and we'll call the police."

"I can't believe you just let him take the money like that," Robin said.

Tony shrugged. "I made a deal with him, and he fulfilled as much of it as he could immediately. I'm like Barry, though. I expect him to be back." He straightened his tie. "Let's catch some dinner. What's the special here tonight, Robin?"

Two hours later, Robin left Tony and Barry at the table to put out a personnel fire in the kitchen. After settling the argument between Casey and a sous chef and soothing the chef's hurt feelings, she went back to the dining room and stopped short, her heart in her throat, when she saw Craig standing next to Tony's table. The two men spoke briefly, then Tony nodded and stood. He gestured with his hand

and they walked in the direction of Robin's office with Craig leading the way.

Robin rushed over to Barry. "What just happened?"

Barry looked as confused as Robin felt. "I have no idea. He just asked if he could talk with Tony alone."

They waited for Tony and Craig to emerge from the office. Customers came and went. Plates came out of the kitchen full and returned empty. The dining room gradually emptied and the staff gradually reset tables and pushed sweepers over the carpet. Still the two men stayed locked away. The kitchen quieted, the last dish put away, the last knife re-sheathed, and the staff left. Robin and Barry waited.

Sitting in the hallway outside of the office, Robin and Barry played a game of Go-Fish while Robin asked Barry faith based questions, trying to learn as much as she could. Hyperintelligent, Barry knew a lot of information right off of the top of his head, and the more questions she asked, the more questions she had.

When the door to the office opened, they surged to their feet. What she saw next left her gaping with her mouth open in surprise. Tony walked out with his arm around Craig's shoulders. The older man's tearstained face practically glowed. She hardly recognized him as the same man.

Tony gestured at Barry. "He'll help you with everything from now on," Tony said.

Barry put his hands in his pockets and raised an eyebrow. "Oh? What's going on, brother?"

"It would seem," Tony said, "that Craig here suffered from some enormous conviction after leaving here. He took the money to Mr. Mills and on the way back to his apartment, he had a breakdown followed by an epiphany."

"I was a sinner," Craig said. "Tony here, he really knows how to pray, and I couldn't get his words out of my mind."

Confused, a little nervous, a little happy, Robin gave a small laugh. "Really?" She smiled at Tony. "I hadn't noticed."

"Craig came back and asked to speak to me privately. When we got to your office, he wanted to know more about God and wanted to understand his conviction."

Tony moved until he could put an arm around Robin's shoulders. "We prayed for quite some time then Craig came to know Christ."

Robin gasped in surprise. "What? Seriously? That's wonderful!"

"The rest of the time was spent worrying about what to do next."

Tony looked at Craig, who nodded and sighed. "I need to turn myself in."

Robin gasped. "No!"

Craig nodded. "I do. I murdered two people, and I've done some things that I ain't proud of no more, but I need to pay for them."

Tony nodded to Barry. "Which is where you come in."

"Of course." The giant pulled a business card out of his pants pocket. "Just call me first thing in the morning. We'll meet and get some things straight before you turn yourself in." As Craig took the card, Barry gripped it a little tighter so that Craig met his eyes. "I mean it. Don't go in without me."

Craig nodded. "I understand." He pocketed the card

and turned toward Robin. "I'm sorry. I'm sorry for everything."

Stunned, Robin nodded her head. "I appreciate that, but I really think that I am just going to have to digest all of this for now."

"That's fair, girl. I understand. I'm going to go stay at Tony's hotel tonight. He gave me a room so that I can stay safe until I meet with Mr. Andersen tomorrow."

"Barry."

Craig accepted the correction. "Until I meet with Barry tomorrow." He turned and hesitated before holding a hand out to Tony. "Thank you."

Tony took the hand to pull him to a hug. "My pleasure, brother. I will see you tomorrow."

After Craig left, Robin leaned against the hallway wall. "Wow."

Tony laughed. "Wow is a word for it, yes." He laughed some more. "Wow."

CHAPTER EIGHTEEN

Robin stood with the water lapping at her ankles while her feet slowly sank into the sand. The sun beat hot against her neck, and the wind blew her cotton skirt around her legs. She took the rubber band out of her braid and slowly loosened her hair, wanting to feel the strands blowing in the breeze.

She felt Tony approach before she heard him or saw him. Some radar inside of her perked up and she slowly turned, a smile on her face.

"I can't believe that it's Christmas Eve," she said. She ran her hands along her bare arms. Bare arms—in December! "Do we even know what the weather report for Boston is today?"

The second he stood close enough to touch, his arm snaked around her waist. She loved the feel of him against her. "I don't check the weather there until I have to go back. I typically avoid it during the winter months."

Forgetting everything but the bliss surrounding her

heart, Robin asked, "Why?"

Tony squeezed her close before releasing her. "I don't like to be cold." He gestured to the mammoth house behind him. "I'm like a bird, I fly south for the winter."

Robin heard a squealing sound of glee and shielded her eyes to look up at the house and see one of the O'Farrell children dive off of the high dive into the pool. They had come to spend Christmas with Tony, and from what Robin could understand, they came every year. An older laugh chased the squeal, and Robin saw Maxine go flying off of the high dive. Obviously, they engaged in some sort of game of tag.

"It looks like you typically carry a flock with you."

Tony grinned. They turned back to look out over the aquamarine water that stretched out beyond his private beach in the Florida Keys. He pulled her closer so she wrapped her arms around his waist and laid her head on his shoulder as they watched a sailboat meander along the horizon.

"Do you row here?"

"Only in my gym." He rested his head against hers and closed his eyes. "I windsurf here."

"That sounds like fun."

"I'll teach you how tomorrow." He squeezed her close then pulled away, running the tips of his fingers down her arm until their hands linked. "Want to take a walk?"

"Sure." She disengaged her feet from the sand and stepped into line with him. "I am so happy that you invited us here. I love it here."

"I do, too." He gestured at the water. "God's design is so perfect. It humbles me when I come here. It's a place for me to come when I start feeling a little too full of myself, a little too big man on the campus. I come here and I look at this expanse and the gloriousness of this perfection and remember that it's all God, and it's all about God."

She stopped and smiled at him. "I love listening to you, especially when you're talking about God."

He turned slightly so that he faced her. "What do you like about me speaking?"

Looking at him in his cotton pants and white cotton short sleeved shirt, his skin dark in the sun, his eyes a rich chocolate brown, she felt her heartbeat pick up its rhythm. She suddenly wanted to kiss him, to keep kissing him, to never have to stop. She felt her tongue dart out, lick suddenly dry lips, as those images started popping up in her mind. "Well," she said, stepping forward so that she could feel the heat from his body. "I love your voice. I love your passion. And," she said, feeling bolder than she had ever felt in her entire life, she reached up and put her hands on his shoulders, "I love the love in your voice when you talk about God."

He put his hands on her hips and smiled a smile that warmed his eyes with a love that took her breath away. "You like my voice, *cara*?"

Grinning she leaned forward and ran her lips along his cheek, feeling for the first time ever, a day's growth of stubble. "Especially when you say words like *cara*."

"Oh?" He swallowed hard. "You like Italian, eh?"

"Yes." She skimmed her lips over his cheek, down his chin, across his neck, and along his other cheek. She could feel his pulse pick up rhythm under her lips. "Very much so."

He cupped her face in his hands and pulled her back just far enough to cover her lips with his own. He kissed her, and she drank him in, tasted him, feeling him seep into her very soul. "How about this?" He said when he broke the contact of their mouths. *"Ti amo con tutto il cuore e con tutta l'anima."*

Robin looked into his eyes and saw the seriousness of whatever he said. She tried to pick through the words, find something that sounded familiar so that she could translate it. Did he just…? "Say it again," she demanded.

"Ti amo con tutto il cuore e con tutta l'anima." She started quaking inside of her stomach. His hands moved from her face down her neck until they rested on her shoulders. "I love you, Robin. With all of my heart and soul."

The quaking left her stomach and radiated out to her limbs. With shaking hands, she cupped his cheeks. "Tony," she said, trying to talk around the huge smile on her face, around the nervous laughter bubbling up in her throat. "I realized I was in love with you the day of your party, but then Craig came and…" she stopped, not wanting to babble incessantly. "Let me try," she said.

He cupped her hands with his and pulled them off of his face. Keeping one hand gripped in his, he stepped back a bit while her inexperienced tongue fumbled on the words. *"Ti amo, con tat,* no," she said, then gasped as he slipped the ring on her finger.

"Con tutto il cuore e con tutta l'anima." He finished for her. Trapping her eyes with his, he slowly descended until one knee rested on the sandy beach. "Marry me, Robin. Make my life complete."

"I—I—" She couldn't tear her eyes off the sapphire.

Tony's face, always so stoic and guarded, could be read

by anyone who saw it. He looked at her with naked need and tender hope. "I love you, *cara*. I don't think that there was a moment in my life that made me happier than the day that you came to know Christ, the day that you gave your life over to the Lord. If you would do me the honor of being my wife…" He stopped and closed his eyes. Holding her hand, he ran his thumb over the ring. "Let me love you in every way God commanded a man to love his wife. Let me treasure you, and abide in you, and protect you, and honor you."

The quaking subsided. Peace flooded her body, warmed her from the inside out. "Yes," she said through the tears that fell unencumbered down her cheeks. He stood and their eyes came back to even again. She laughed and grabbed him and hugged him. "Yes, of course. Of course I'll be your wife."

He wrapped both of his arms around her and hugged her tightly to him, lifting her up from the sand and spinning them both around until he felt the wet surf beneath his feet. As he gently returned her to earth, his lips found hers and they kissed, standing in the sand with the water swirling at their ankles.

THE END

TRANSLATION KEY

amica—female friend

aspetto—be looking forward to; expectation

bello—beautiful

buona sera—good evening

cara—dear (beloved, darling)

cara mia—my dear

ciao—hello or good-bye

il mio amico—male friend, buddy

Ti ringrazio, Dio—thank you, God

mi amico—my friend

mio fratello—my brother

mise en place—French culinary term 'everything in place'

si un piccolo testardo—a little stubborn (pig-headed)

ti amo con tutto il cuore e con tutta l'anima—I love you with all of my heart and soul

DISCUSSION QUESTIONS

Suggested group discussion questions for *Sapphire Ice*.

When asking ourselves how important the truth is to our Creator, we can look to the reason Jesus said he was born. In the book of John 18:37, Jesus explains that for this reason He was born and for this reason He came into the world. The reason? To testify to the truth.

> Pilate therefore said to Him, "Are You a king then?"
> Jesus answered, "You say *rightly* that I am a king. For this cause I was born, and for this cause I have come into the world, that I should bear witness [*testify*] to the truth. Everyone who is of the truth hears My voice."
> John 18:37 (NKJV)

In bringing those He ministered to into an understanding of the truth, Our Lord used fiction in the form of parables to illustrate very real truths. In the same way, we can minister to one another by the use of fictional characters and situations to help us to reach logical, valid, cogent, and very sound conclusions about our real lives here on earth.

While the characters and situations in **The Jewel Series** are fictional, I pray that these extended parables can help readers come to a better understanding of truth. Please prayerfully consider the questions that follow, consult scripture, and pray upon your conclusions. May the Lord of the universe richly bless you.

The sisters suffer a terrible childhood in an always unsafe environment. Too young, they know hunger, exposure, deprivation, and want. They know the dangers and evils of the world and are exposed to the very worst mankind has to offer. It is easy to pontificate that a loving God would not allow children to suffer like that, but the truth is that the very finest vessels are put through the fire several times.

1. To which sister do you most relate? What is it about her personality that makes you relate to her?

2. Is there something in your childhood you feel certain molded and shaped your adult world view especially with respect to relationships?

3. Do you think the sisters would be very different as adults if their childhood upbringing were positively different?

Barry cautioned Tony not to see Robin because she wasn't saved. Read 2 Corinthians 6:14 to see what the Bible says.

4. Are you in an evenly yoked relationship or are you spiritually on the same path? What are some evidences you can name?

Sarah has a burden lifted when Tony offers to fund her church's fall carnival. Many churches today could widen the outreach of their various ministries but they suffer from lack of funding.

5. Why do you believe churches have such a hard time finding funding for ministries? How can you help your church overcome such common issues?

Robin didn't believe in a just and loving God because she had seen and experienced the worst life has to offer.

6. How do you think desolation or tragedy relates to God?

7. Do you believe God wants us to lean on Him and look to Him in all things in life? How much of Robin's desire to "do it on her own" do you believe might have kept her separated from God?

Robin knew nothing about God and had a very low

opinion of Christians in general. This despite the fact that she grew up in a neighborhood with a very large and very active church right in the middle of it. She later confesses that she remembers that church as one of her childhood landmarks.

8. What can we do to better spread the word of God in a positive light among unbelievers?

Read Matthew 6:14 and Matthew 18:22. Put the meaning of these verses about forgiveness in your own words.

9. What was your reaction to Tony and Robin's treatment of Craig at the end of Sapphire Ice?

10. Are you currently coping with unforgiveness in your heart?

S uggested **luncheon menu for** a group discussion about *Sapphire Ice*.

Those who follow my Hallee the Homemaker website know that one thing I am passionate about in life is selecting, cooking, and savoring good whole real food. A special luncheon just goes hand in hand with hospitality and ministry.

In case you're planning a discussion group surrounding this book, I offer some humble suggestions to help your special luncheon talk come off as a success. Quick as you like, you can whip up an appetizer, salad, entree and dessert that is sure to please and certain to enhance your discussion and time of friendship and fellowship.

The appetizer:

BENEDICT'S PARMESEAN ARTICHOKE DIP

Readers ask about an artichoke dip tasty enough that Sarah's mother, Darlene Thomas, would request it for a party even if as a point of pride it arrives by way of her nemesis Robin Bartlett.

This recipe is *so* yummy, especially when the baguettes are still toasty warm. I pray it blesses you.

ℐNGREDIENTS

1 Baguette loaf

Extra virgin olive oil

2 garlic cloves

1 14-ounce can artichoke hearts in water

6 ounces cream cheese, softened

$^1/_4$ cup Greek yogurt

$^1/_4$ cup mayonnaise

$^1/_2$ cup grated fresh Parmesan cheese

$^1/_2$ teaspoon red pepper flakes

$^1/_4$ teaspoon salt

$^1/_4$ teaspoon garlic powder

𝒫REPARATION

Slice the Baguette into $^1/_2$ inch diagonal slices. Using a pastry brush, lightly brush olive oil on each slice.

Broil on the top rack of the oven until brown. Rub each toasted piece lightly with a garlic clove.

Preheat oven to 350° degrees F (180° degrees C).

Drain the artichoke hearts and roughly chop.

DIRECTIONS

Beat the cream cheese until fluffy. Stir in the yogurt and mayonnaise. Stir in the cheese and spices. Mix with the artichoke hearts.

Pour into a pie plate and bake for 25 to 30 minutes, or until bubbly.

Let cool and serve with the Baguette toast.

The Salad:

SARAH'S STRAWBERRY SPINACH SALAD

Chef Casey at Hank's Place knows just how to please Sarah's vegetarian palate with this wonderful vegan friendly, Daniel fast friendly offering.

INGREDIENTS

10 ounces fresh spinach leaves

1 quart strawberries

$1/2$ cup mandarin orange slices

$1/2$ cup pecan halves

1 TBS sunflower seeds

$1/4$ cup balsamic vinegar

$1/2$ cup extra virgin olive oil

$1/2$ tsp salt (Kosher or sea salt is best)

$1/4$ tsp fresh ground black pepper

℘REPARATION

Thoroughly wash and drain the spinach leaves. Tear into bite sized pieces.

Wash, hull, and halve the strawberries.

Roughly chop the pecans

ⅅIRECTIONS

Place the spinach in a large salad bowl. Top with the strawberries and orange slices. Sprinkle with the pecan halves and the sunflower seeds.

In a small bowl, whisk together the oil, vinegar, salt, and pepper until emulsified. Pour over the salad and lightly toss.

Serve immediately.

The Entrée:

VISCOLLI'S VERMICCELLI WITH GARDEN VEGETABLES

The Boston Viscolli Hotels are well known for 5-star international cuisine and the specialty is always, no surprise, Italian fare.

ℐNGREDIENTS

1 pound Vermicelli

1 TBS extra virgin olive oil

1 tsp salt (Kosher or sea salt is best)

1 TBS extra virgin olive oil

1 small onion

2 cloves garlic

1 large or 2 small carrot

1 zucchini

1 yellow squash

1 can diced tomatoes

1 tsp honey (local raw is best)

2 tsp dried oregano

2 tsp dried parsley

1 tsp dried basil

1 tsp salt (Kosher or sea salt is best)

$^1/_2$ tsp fresh ground pepper

PREPARATION

Slice the onion. Mince the garlic. Thinly slice the carrot. Slice the zucchini and squash.

DIRECTIONS

Bring a pot of pure water to boil. Add 1 TBS olive oil and 1 tsp salt. Add Vermicelli. If store bought, cook according to package directions.

Heat a large skillet over medium-high heat. Add 1 TBS extra virgin olive oil. Add the sliced onion. Cook about 5 minutes or until it starts to get tender.

Add the garlic and the carrots. Cook about 5 minutes.

Add the zucchini, squash, and canned tomatoes. Gently

stir in the spices, salt, and pepper.

Bring to a gentle boil. Reduce heat and cover. Let cook for about 10 minutes.

Place the cooked pasta on a large platter. Top with the sauce. Serve with fresh ground parmesan cheese, if desired.

The Dessert:

MAXINE'S MARVELOUS MARBLE CAKE

When Maxine invites Tony to stay and celebrate his birthday, she makes him Maxine's Marvelous Marble cake which brightens his day.

ℐNGREDIENTS

1 $^1/_2$ cups butter, softened

1 $^3/_4$ cups granulated sugar

6 large eggs

1 tsp vanilla extract

2 $^2/_3$ cup flour

4 tsp aluminum-free baking powder.

$^1/_2$ tsp salt (Kosher or sea salt is best)

$^1/_2$ cup whole milk

3 TBS baking cocoa powder

confectioner's sugar, for dusting.

𝒫REPARATION

Preheat the oven to 350° degrees F (180° degrees C). Butter and flour a Bundt pan. tapping out the excess flour.

Sift together the flour, baking powder, and salt. Set aside. Mix the milk and the vanilla. Set aside.

*D*IRECTIONS

With an electric mixer, beat the butter and sugar on high for 3 minutes. Add the eggs one at a time, beating well after each addition.

Add about half of the dry mixture and beat on low speed. Add the milk mixture and beat on low speed until mixed. Add the remaining flour and beat until just mixed.

Spoon one-third of the batter into the pan. Transfer half the remaining

batter into another bowl and sift in the cocoa powder. Mix well.

Spoon dallops of the chocolate batter into the pan. Top with the remaining plain batter. Use a knife to gently swirl the two batters together to create a marble pattern. Be careful not to mix it too much.

Bake for 45 minutes, or until a toothpick inserted into the center comes out clean.

Cool the cake for 10 minutes before removing from the pan. When cooled completely, dust with powdered sugar.

The Jewel Series by Hallee Bridgeman

Book 1: *Sapphire Ice*, a novel

Book 2: *Greater Than Rubies*, a novella

Book 3: *Emerald Fire*, a novel

Book 4: *Topaz Heat*, a novel

Book 5: *Christmas Diamond*, a novella

Book 6: *Christmas Star Sapphire*, a novella

Enjoy this special excerpt from book 2 in this series.

Robin clutched the bag in her hand a little tighter as the elevator came to a stop. She stepped out into the lobby of Tony's executive offices. The receptionist was speaking into her headset, so she just lifted her hand in a greeting and walked to Tony's office.

Her stomach twisted itself into painful knots, and she could barely breathe. As she got closer to the double doors leading to his outer office, she felt like they lay suddenly farther away. A cold sweat broke out on her upper lip.

She'd dressed carefully this morning, choosing a long navy blue pencil skirt and gray cashmere sweater. Now she wished she'd worn something cooler, or maybe layers so she could shed some heat. Thankfully, she'd thought to pin her hair up, so at least that wasn't suffocating her.

She noticed the tremble in her hand as she opened the door and stepped into Margaret's office.

Margaret stood as Robin entered." Hello, Robin. Mr. Viscolli will be happy to see you," she said, moving around her desk to open the large door leading to Tony's inner sanctuary.

Not for long, she thought, but merely smiled and put a shaking hand to her stomach.

Tony stood next to his desk, sorting papers. His suit jacket was draped on the chair behind him. He wore a white shirt with a blue and black striped tie. When he looked up, he had a distracted frown on his face, but when his eyes met Robin's, his features immediately relaxed and he smiled.

"*Cara mia*," he said, setting the stack of papers down and coming around his desk. "What an unexpected pleasure. Nothing could have surprised or pleased me more."

Robin did not hear Margaret shut the door behind her. Her heart started pounding and nausea churned in her gut. As Tony walked forward, she had to resist the urge to step backward. When he was just a few feet away from her, he did not step any closer, nor did he reach out to her.

"What happened?" he asked, his eyes searching her face.

Robin gripped the twine handle of the bag so tightly that she was surprised it didn't cut her skin. "Can we sit?" She gestured at the leather sofa.

"Yes. Of course. Are you ill? What's wrong?" Tony put a hand on her elbow as they moved to the sitting area. Robin fought the urge to lean into him and let him make everything okay. When she was with him, it seemed like it would definitely always be okay. But in her heart, she knew that was a false sense of security.

He sat on the couch, and she perched on the edge of the couch, turning her body toward him. With a shaking hand, she wiped the sweat off of her lip. "I—" Her breath hiccupped, but she forced forward and refused to give in to tears. If she cried, he would put his arms around her, and she would lose all strength to go forward with this.

He reached for her hand, sandwiching it between both of his. "Your hands are freezing," he said, concerned.

"Tony," she whispered, "I can't marry you."

FICTION BOOKS BY HALLEE

Find the latest information and connect with Hallee at her website: www.halleebridgeman.com

The Virtues and Valor series:

Book 1: Temperance's Trial
Book 2: Homeland's Hope
Book 3: Charity's Code
Book 4: A Parcel for Prudence
Book 5: Grace's Ground War
Book 6: Mission of Mercy
Book 7: Flight of Faith
Book 8: Valor's Vigil

The Song of Suspense Series:

Book 1: A Melody for James
Book 2: An Aria for Nick
Book 3: A Carol for Kent
Book 4: A Harmony for Steve

Standalone Suspense:

On The Ropes

PARODY COOKBOOKS BY HALLEE

Vol 1: Fifty Shades of Gravy, a Christian gets Saucy!
Vol 2: The Walking Bread, the Bread Will Rise
Vol 3: Iron Skillet Man, the Stark Truth about Pepper and Pots
Vol 4: Hallee Crockpotter & the Chamber of Sacred Ingredients

THE DIXON BROTHERS SERIES
COMING IN 2018

Find the latest information and connect with Hallee at her website: www.halleebridgeman.com

Courting Calla: Dixon Brothers book 1

Ian knows God has chosen Calla as the woman for him, but Calla is hiding something big. Can Calla trust Ian with her secret, or will she let it destroy any possible hope for a future they may have?

Valerie's Virdict: Dixon Brothers book 2

Since boyhood days, Brad has always carried a flame for Valerie. Her engagement to another man shattered his dreams. When she comes home, battered and bruised, recovering from a nearly fatal relationship, he prays God will use him to help her heal.

Alexandra's Appeal: Dixon Brothers book 3

Jon falls very quickly in love with Alex's zest for life and her perspective of the the world around her. He steps off of his path to be with her. When forces move against them and rip them apart, he wants to believe God will bring them back together, but it might take a miracle.

Daisy's Decision: Dixon Brothers book 4

Daisy has had a crush on Ken since high school, so going on just one date with him can't possibly hurt, can it? Even if she's just been painfully dumped by the man she planned to spend the rest of her life with, and whose unborn baby she carries? Just one date?

With more than half a million  sales and more than 20 books in print, Hallee Bridgeman is a best-selling Christian author who writes romance and action-packed romantic suspense focusing on realistic characters who face real world problems. Her work has been described as everything from refreshingly realistic to heart-stopping exciting and edgy.

A prolific writer, when she's not penning novels, you will find her in the kitchen, which she considers the "heart of the home." Her passion for cooking spurred her to launch a whole food, real food "Parody" cookbook series. In addition to nutritious, Biblically grounded recipes, readers will find that each cookbook also confronts some controversial aspect of secular pop culture.

Hallee loves coffee, campy action movies, and regular date nights with her husband. Above all else, she loves God with all of her heart, soul, mind, and strength; has been redeemed by the blood of Christ; and relies on the presence of the Holy Spirit to guide her. She prays her work here on earth is a blessing to you and would love to hear from you.

You can reach Hallee via the CONTACT link on her website or send an email to hallee@halleebridgeman.com.

Newsletter Sign Up: tinyurl.com/HalleeNews/

Author Site: www.halleebridgeman.com

Facebook: www.facebook.com/pages/Hallee-Bridgeman/192799110825012

Twitter: twitter.com/halleeb

NEWSLETTER

Hallee News Letter
http://tinyurl.com/HalleeNews/

Sign up for Hallee's monthly newsletter! Every newsletter recipient is automatically entered into a monthly giveaway! The real prize is you will never miss updates about upcoming releases, book signings, appearances, or other events.

CPSIA information can be obtained
at www.ICGtesting.com
Printed in the USA
FFHW021119241119
56111941-62189FF